At Home
with Ben and Gretchen

When Normal Is No Longer Normal

by

Kathy Carman Henderson

This book is a work of fiction. Some real locations are mentioned in the book, but what takes place there, and the people involved, are not real. Any relationship to people, living or dead, is coincidental.

Cover photo is by the author.

DEDICATION

To people who care for others through difficult times.

Characters:

Anna – Gretchen & Ben Parks' daughter
Anthony – student member of school problem solving group
Cliffy Barrows – preschool boy living close to the Parks
Brittany – student member of school problem solving group
Chairman Buchanan – leader of Quad Cities United Mission
      Group
Dorine Carmine – widowed neighbor of Parks
Chip – one of SDMC School's custodians
Claire's – lunch counter close to SDMC School
Flora – Parks' granddaughter, Anna's daughter
Mr. Grabel – instrumental music teacher at South Des
      Moines County School where Gretchen Parks teaches
Ethel Gunther – Gretchen Park's mom
Herman Gunther – Ethel's husband, Gretchen's father
Hoovers – pastor small church in Silvis, IL
Ted Jones – very liberal member of QCUMG
Janella – Good art student and part of problem solving team
Grandma Kelly – Janella's grandmother from Chicago
Lenny – long-time custodian at SDMC School
Brother Manuel – leads Kansas City storefront church
Brother Moses Martin – very conservative member of
      QCUMG
Mark – Parks' son-in-law, Anna's husband
Mary – school secretary
Dr. Mertz – the Parks' family physician
Principal Mitchell – principal of SDMC School
Mabel Morgan – Dorine Carmine's little sister
Betsy Moth – Social Studies & problem solving teacher at
      SDMC School
Jeremy Munch – Janella's stepdad
Ben Parks – Midwestern Baptist pastor married to Gretchen
Gretchen Parks – Ben's wife and an elementary art teacher
QCUMG – Quad Cities United Missions Group, a group
      formed by small churches to work on missions projects
Sylvia – Ethel Gunther's neighbor in Kansas City

CHAPTER 1

"Ma! Mama!" Gretchen shouted. She positioned herself at the corner of the yard and looked in every direction. There was no sign of anyone except Cliffy Barrows playing with his dog in his backyard. Where could her mother have gone?

As Gretchen turned, she thought back over the short time since her mother had come to stay with them.

Ethel Gunther stood by the tracks when Gretchen and Ben's train pulled into the Kansas City station on the way home from the Grand Canyon. Ethel's young neighbor gave her a hug and handed Ethel's bags to the conductor as she stepped onto the train. Gretchen had asked the conductor if she could come down with the people who were disembarking, so she was just inside the car's entrance. Though Ethel officially had a seat in the coach car, Gretchen led her mother carefully through that car and the next to the small compartment she and her husband Ben were occupying.

That trip to the Grand Canyon had been planned at about the same time as Gretchen's mom's visit. So, they were meeting her on their return. Ethel clutched her daughter's hand as she stepped gingerly over the connection between train cars. Gretchen was moving her mother as quickly as she could, hoping to reach the sleeper compartment before the train started.

Just as she felt the first lurch of the starting train, she saw Ben's head stick out through a doorway about ten feet ahead. "Hold onto the walls, Mom," coached Gretchen. "We're almost there."

"Okay," murmured Ethel, obediently pressing one hand against the wall of the narrow hallway. The other clutched several spiral notebooks. She followed Gretchen until she was safely inside the mini-room, where Gretchen motioned her mother to the empty seat, taking a place opposite her, snuggled in next to her husband.

Looking a little stressed, Ethel glanced out the window. "Why, look at that!" she exclaimed. "There's my neighbor! Is she getting on the train too?"

Ben reached over and patted his mother-in-law's arm. "Mother Gunther, she brought you down to the train."

"Well, wasn't that nice of her!" exclaimed Ethel. "You know, I don't know how I would have gotten here without her help. She has been a very good neighbor."

"She sure has," responded Gretchen, looking concerned.

"I gave her my laptop," added Ethel.

Ben smiled. "That was a thoughtful thing to do."

"Well, there's not much to look at outside the window," Ethel continued as they rolled through Kansas City. "But I'm going to enjoy my ride with you!"

Gretchen smiled, then realized there was something else she needed to check. "Mom, did you take your pills this morning? Have you had breakfast?"

Ethel looked thoughtful. "Let me see… I feel a little hungry, but… wait... let me check my purse." She opened her large bag and pulled out a pillbox divided into fourteen sections. "What day is today?"

"Tuesday," replied Ben.

Ethel pointed to the third section of the pill container. "I've taken my morning pills."

Just then Gretchen's cell phone rang. "Hi, Mrs. Parks, this is Sylvia, Ethel's neighbor."

"Yes, Sylvia, thank you so much for helping Mom make it to the train."

"No prob. I thought you might want to know – Ethel took her pills with some milk this morning. You'd said something about breakfast on the train."

"Yes, I did. Thanks for the information. It's helpful."

"Sure, Mrs. Parks. Hope you have a nice trip."

"Thanks, bye."

Gretchen turned to her mom. "That was your neighbor. She said you'd taken your pills – but you'd already told me that. She also said that you hadn't eaten anything except a glass of milk."

"Well, then it's time to head for the dining car!" declared Ben.

Ben exited the car first, holding one of Ethel's hands to lead her. Gretchen brought up the rear. Ben pulled and Gretchen pushed gently when Ethel stood before the car connection. With an uncertain leap, Ethel landed almost in her son-in-law's arms. Ben moved backwards, taking Ethel with him, and Gretchen made it across the shifting teeth between the cars.

A young man, dressed in uniform approached. "Table for three?"

All three nodded.

This time Gretchen sat next to her mother, with Ben on the opposite side of the table.

"What would you like?" a young woman, also in uniform, asked a few minutes later.

Ben motioned to the ladies to go first. Gretchen glanced at her mother and got a vacant look in return. She turned back to the waitress. "I'll have the oatmeal with raisins and brown sugar. And milk."

The waitress looked at Ethel. She smiled sweetly up at her. "I'll have what she's having," said Ethel nodding toward her daughter.

Gretchen blinked. She didn't remember her mom being particularly fond of oatmeal.

Ben opted for the omelet with bacon and coffee. The waitress nodded and left the table.

Ethel looked around, continuing to smile. "This is so nice! A restaurant right on the train!" She glanced at Ben and Gretchen and continued a little more softly. "And I'm here with two of my favorite people on earth."

Gretchen gave her mother a little hug, then turned to look

out the window. Just for a second, she blinked back tears. Her mother's mind had failed quite a bit since she had seen her last. From these few minutes with her, Gretchen doubted that her mother would ever be able to live alone again. But – Gretchen got hold of her emotions – she was here, happy to be with them, and Gretchen was going to enjoy this time.

Ethel was looking out the window also. "Those trees are going by awfully fast."

Ben agreed. "We'll get home quickly at this speed."

"Not before we get our breakfast, I hope."

Gretchen chuckled at her mom's joke. Memory might be going, but Ethel still had her sense of humor. "Breakfast should be here soon."

It wasn't over a minute before the waitress came down the aisle toward them with a heavily laden tray. She served Ben his food first, and his coffee. Next, she set out the two milks and the two oatmeal bowls, followed by small containers of brown sugar and raisins. Ethel stared at her bowl. "Oatmeal? Hmm. Well, they brought plenty of brown sugar…"

Gretchen was both amused and concerned. Apparently her mother couldn't remember that she had ordered the oatmeal. Maybe she hadn't even been aware that that was what Gretchen had ordered. She watched Ethel drown her oatmeal with melting brown sugar, then turned to drizzle raisins and sugar over her own.

After all had eaten their fill, Gretchen guided her mother to the restroom; then they settled back into their cabin. It wasn't more than a minute or two before Ethel drifted off to sleep. Gretchen leaned her head on Ben's shoulder and allowed herself to sleep also.

Just a few hours later Gretchen helped her mother into their home in Western Central Illinois. Ben got the bags.

"We've got things ready for you, Mom. We've turned the dining room into a bedroom for you… see, we've brought Calvin's bed down and his old dresser. There's a comfy chair for you next to your bed, and a nightstand you can keep things in."

Ethel settled into the chair while Gretchen continued, "You see right through that door? That's the kitchen. Go in there and you'll find our downstairs bathroom on the left. We made space in the bathroom drawer for your things. And we bought one of those shower stools, so if you get tired you can sit down while you're showering."

Ethel nodded. Ben came in with Ethel's bags and Gretchen helped her put her things away. Leaving her mother looking out a window at birds in the backyard, Gretchen turned to help Ben bring in and put away their things. As she came down the stairs from her own bedroom, Gretchen noticed her mother wandering around the living room. "Hi, Mom,"

Ethel looked up at her. "Hi, girl." She paused for a moment. Gretchen had the distinct impression that she was thinking something through. "You're home here is very comfortable." She smiled over at Gretchen as she came off the stairs. "I do need to ask where the little girls' room is, however."

Gretchen started slightly. "Here, Mom, I'll show you." She took her mom back through her bedroom and into the kitchen. Pointing to the half-open bathroom door, Gretchen saw Ethel make the connection and head that way. She turned around to see Ben standing there.

"Didn't you explain where the bathroom was earlier?" asked Ben.

Gretchen nodded.

"Hmm." Ben said no more. He moved to an end table with a drawer in it. Opening the drawer he pulled out a piece of paper and a marker. As Ben bent over the paper, Gretchen got out a roll of tape from the same drawer and started rolling pieces to stick on the back of Ben's makeshift sign. By the time Ethel opened the bathroom door, they had a sign posted on the kitchen door to help her next time.

By bedtime that evening Gretchen found herself exhausted. Her mother seemed quite disoriented; would she have to stay with her every minute? As Gretchen lay there staring at the dark ceiling, Ben whispered in her ear, "It may get better when she gets used to things, Gretchen. Today Mom was out of her element. When this becomes her place, she may be okay."

Gretchen leaned her head toward him. "You're saying we'll keep her here."

Ben stroked her cheek. "Don't you think we need to?"

"I'm wondering how we can…"

Ben sighed. "You only work half time. I can adjust hours; Mom can go with me, if needed, to some things."

Gretchen found his hand and squeezed it. "Just what we need. More unexpected adventures."

Ben chuckled. "That's life."

Gretchen added, "At least for us," as she rolled into her husband's shoulder.

"Lord, give us a good night's sleep so that we can function well tomorrow," prayed Ben. Gretchen nodded and, hearing a gentle snoring start almost immediately, added more to the prayer silently.

As the next few days went by, Gretchen began to think Ben might be right. Her mother began to settle into the routine of their lives. They learned to leave the makings of her breakfast out on the counter so that she could find it if she awoke first in the morning. She learned to look for signs and use cues to find what she needed. Gretchen and Ben put more and more little labels around.

The very next morning, Gretchen called her family doctor in Burlington and asked for an appointment for her mother. The appointment was made for the following week, which would give Gretchen time to look over the papers her mother had brought and be able to add her own observations to the conversation with her doctor. The only thing that concerned Gretchen about the delay in seeing the doctor was that it was the day before she was supposed to report back to school. If there were any other appointments… Well, it was best to take one day at a time.

Morning and evening Gretchen and her mother took long walks together. Gretchen tried to point out landmarks, but wasn't sure whether these were making an impression. What was precious to both of them was the talks they had during these walks. They talked about family, Gretchen doing most of the talking, but Ethel occasionally telling a family story that Gretchen had never heard before. She wondered whether her mother's memories were accurate, but accurate or not, they usually were delivered with wit and a real understanding of human nature. Gretchen knew that she would remember these walks at least until such a time as she was in the same condition as her mom.

Sunday came, and though Ethel seemed a little overwhelmed by her warm welcome by parishioners, she seemed to enjoy the church service. Ben included one of her favorite hymns, and she had no problem singing all the verses without looking either at a hymnal or the overhead projection.

Monday was similar to the days of the previous week, except that Gretchen made a point of sitting down with Ethel and studying the papers she had brought from her Kansas City specialists. She felt a catch in her chest as she began to understand what she was looking at. One paper listed her mother's physical problems: hardening of the arteries, high blood pressure, a tendency toward digestive difficulties common to senior citizens. Then there was the mental function report: evidence of moderate dementia possibly related to blood flow, but also shown by brain shrinkage in an MRI. Also, a part of her brain seemed to have been damaged at some time in the past, a part of her brain that would relate to decision making. Gretchen turned to her mother's prescription list. Donepezil. Gretchen recognized the medication most commonly used for Alzheimer's. There was another she recognized for high blood pressure; Ben took that one. There was one for bladder issues, and a couple she had no clue what they were for. Gretchen took a deep breath. How could Mom have functioned on her own with all of these problems? She was going to have to contact that young neighbor to thank her; it looks like she had done a lot more than her mother had told her. She probably deserved to be paid much more than a second-hand computer for her troubles.

The next day was the doctor's appointment. Gretchen made sure that she and her mom had time for their walk before they went. It was an unusually cool morning, so Gretchen helped her mom into her sweater, asked her if she needed to take a bathroom break before they left, and then waited while she did just that. She stood at the kitchen door, so her mom would see her as soon as she came out.

Her mom followed her to the door and passed through it, as Gretchen held it open. Gazing around with a big smile on her face, Ethel said, "What a wonderful day! Oh, Gretchen, look at the birds! Look at those bright yellow ones bouncing through the air!"

"Yes, they are pretty, aren't they Mom. Those are goldfinches. There are quite a few of them around here."

"Most birds don't bounce like that when they fly. Why do they do that?"

"Don't know, Mom. But it's cute when they do."

"I agree."

They walked out to the street and turned left. Down at the corner they saw Mrs. Dorine Carmine sweeping her walk.

"Good morning, Mrs. Carmine," said Gretchen.

Mrs. Carmine responded, "Good morning, Gretchen, Ethel. Good morning for a walk."

"Wow! You know my name!" Ethel commented. "I don't know if I'll ever remember yours."

Mrs. Carmine smiled. "That's okay. It's still good to see you."

"And it's good to see you," replied Ethel.

Turning left again at the corner, they continued walking. Cliffy Barrows was pedaling his trike down the street, and Ethel waved at him.

Cliffy waved back. "What a sweet little boy," said Ethel.

"I agree, Mom. You will see him at church too."

"Oh, good!"

At the end of two blocks, a cornfield bordered the far side of the street. Gretchen and Ethel turned left once again. Ethel studied the corn. "What tall corn!"

"Yes, the corn has grown well this year."

"They plant it awfully close together."

"They sure do."

"We were always able to walk both ways through our corn when I was growing up."

"I know, Mom. Everything is done by machine now. No walking through this corn."

An animal dodged into a tunnel in the ditch alongside the road. "A groundhog!" declared Ethel.

Gretchen smiled and nodded.

As they finished their walk, the conversation turned to other memories.

"Mom, do you remember that old draft horse Grandpa used to have?"

"I sure do. It could drag a plow places a tractor couldn't go."

"He didn't use it much for his big fields, did he?"

"Not practical. But it meant he could plant a family garden on the terraced hill behind our house."

"The giant steps, we kids used to call it."

Ethel smiled. "I remember. I can remember helping my mother pick corn and beans from that garden, then shucking corn and snapping beans while Mother got the canning jars sterilized."

"What was your favorite part of living on a farm, Mom?"

"Oh, my! I'm not sure... I think it might have been the smells."

"The smells, Mom? Which ones?"

"This may sound strange, but I liked all of them: the smell of growing things... the musty earth... the sweet smell of fresh straw... the sour smell of old straw that has been covered up for a long time. Even the smell of manure. It all seemed like part of living."

Gretchen smiled. They were back home. "Here we are, Mom."

"Oh... I didn't recognize the house."

"We've got just enough time to get your records and insurance cards together for the doctor's appointment."

"Okay, Gretchen." Ethel followed her daughter into the house and over to the dresser holding her things. She let Gretchen sift through her papers, but noticed that her daughter paused when she got to the group of spiral notebooks. "Those are my… ah… diaries, Gretchen; but they aren't meant to be private."

Gretchen turned to look at her mother, a question in her eyes.

"Oh, I know some people write secret diaries, but I know I have memory problems. I am writing down what I can while I can. I think of you and the rest of my family and hope that this will help some day."

Gretchen's eyebrows rose. She turned back to the dresser. "That's for another day, Mom… but thanks." She straightened the group of papers she'd put on top of the dresser, then closed the drawer. "Let's go!"

"Okay, girl," responded Ethel enthusiastically. "Where did you say we were going?"

Gretchen and her mom went through the preliminaries with a nurse, and had time to discuss the wall illustrations before Dr. Mertz came in. "Hello." He smiled at Ethel. "Whom do I have the honor of seeing today?"

Ethel smiled back. "I'm Ethel Gunther."

He reached out and shook Ethel's hand. "I don't think we've met before."

Ethel glanced at Gretchen. Hesitantly she began, "I don't think so… I've lived in Kansas City until recently."

Dr. Mertz nodded. "I see. Where are you living now?"

Ethel glanced again at Gretchen. "I – I'm not sure. I've been staying with my daughter…"

Gretchen gave Dr. Mertz a questioning glance. He smiled and gave a little sideways shake of his head. Gretchen wasn't sure what that meant, but she thought it might mean she was supposed to keep quiet.

"Oh, I know Gretchen lives on the other side of the river, in Illinois a few miles. What did you think of the Great River Bridge?"

Ethel looked confused. "The bridge… well, it was fine."

"It's relatively new, you know. I think it opened in '93. Let's see, that would make it…" Dr. Mertz looked expectantly at Ethel.

Ethel laughed. "You're going to have to tell me what year it is now, if you want me to work that math problem," she responded.

He told her and she instantly gave him the correct answer. Dr. Mertz nodded appreciatively. "Can I ask you to do another math problem, Ethel?"

Ethel looked at him slyly. "Are you trying to test my brain, Mr. Doctor?"

He grinned.

"I only have half a brain left, I think. But you're free to try to figure out which half."

Dr. Mertz nodded. "Can you count backwards by threes from twenty?"

"Twenty, seventeen, fourteen, eleven, eight, five, two."

"That part of your brain works." He paused. "Can you tell me where you were born?"

"On a farm outside of Tonganoxie, Kansas."

He nodded.

"What's your daughter's name?"

"Gretchen."

He nodded. "Last name?"

"Gunther... no... uh..." she looked confused again.

"It's okay, Mom."

"Well, we found a small glitch, but you know who she is, Ethel." That from the doctor. He glanced down at his paper. "One more question. Can you remember when the bridge was built?"

Ethel shook her head. "If you said, I wasn't paying attention."

"That's fine." Dr. Mertz said. "All this stuff your Kansas City doctors have already checked, but I like to double check myself with a new patient." He smiled and sat down on a stool.

Dr. Mertz smiled gently across at Ethel and spoke. "Well, dear lady, you've been through quite a bit lately, haven't you?"

Ethel shrugged. "That's life."

Dr. Mertz chuckled. "It certainly is." He shuffled through the papers in front of him, most were the ones brought to him, but some his nurse had written when doing the preliminary exam.

"Most of this you know, but I'll review it so we all are on the same page."

Gretchen and Ethel nodded.

"Ethel, you were the caregiver for your husband for several years…"

Ethel nodded.

"As often happens to caregivers, you found it hard to find time for yourself."

Ethel shrugged.

"The stress of caring for Mr. Gunther may have contributed to your developing high blood pressure. Maybe not, but it happened about the same time. It went undetected until you had a few mini-strokes and experienced a little confusion which led your neighbor to take you to a quick care center."

"That girl was a big help in many ways," responded Ethel.

Dr. Mertz nodded. "You've also had several falls. With falls it's sometimes hard to know if later problems were caused by the fall or if the problems caused you to fall. Either way, you've got a problem."

Ethel looked a little worried and so did Gretchen.

Turning to Gretchen, Dr. Mertz continued, "Gretchen, the first thing I want to tell you is not to feel guilty. Ethel contacted you when she was ready to receive your help. She was in familiar circumstances, and she had a good neighbor." He turned toward Ethel. "It's just the last few months that things started getting hard for you, and you started looking at your options."

That night after all were tucked into bed, Gretchen turned to her husband. Suddenly the tears came. Ben moved to put his arms around his wife. "I'm sorry," sobbed Gretchen. "I thought I was taking everything in stride."

"It was a day filled with tension for you, Gretchen. It's okay to feel sadness, or just exhaustion, after a day like this."

"It was the words *assisted living facility* that got to me," replied Gretchen. "Somehow it felt like suggesting *prison* for Mom."

Ben's arms tightened around Gretchen.

"I know it's not. I know these… these places… are much better than they used to be."

"They are the best option for some people."

Another sob escaped Gretchen's lips.

"We won't solve this tonight, Gretchen."

Gretchen sniffed. "I know. You've got tomorrow with Mom while I go to school."

"Yes, after that maybe we can talk about what we can and can't do, either with or without your mom being included in the conversation."

Gretchen nodded. She sat up, reached for a tissue, and heartily blew her nose. "That's a good idea. Mom's tucked in for the night and so are we. Just be sure to pray that I can put this in God's hands and leave it there until the right time to talk about it."

Ben chuckled. "That'll take a miracle on God's part."

CHAPTER 2

Wednesday was the day that Gretchen returned to school for the first teacher workday. Gretchen ate breakfast with her mom, kissed her cheek, and told her she would see her before suppertime.

As Gretchen drove over the Great River Bridge into Burlington, Iowa, she found herself praying, "Lord, help me trust Mom to you today. I know Ben will do his best, but I've started feeling responsible for her in the last several days. And you know how I was with my kids… How I still am with some of my students." Gretchen chuckled as she took the exit onto Highway 61 South, "Yes, I have been learning this summer just how much help from others *I* need to get things done. I'm just glad you let me have a little part in fixing a few problems." She flipped on her favorite radio station as she continued south of the town.

It wasn't too long before she pulled her car into the long parking lot that fronted the equally long building of South Des Moines County School. She pulled past the new end with the gym and cafeteria and down close to the main entrance. Usually she went in the gym entrance, the shortest way to her classroom. However, today she wanted to check her school mailbox and – and she was remembering that she no longer had her room. She pursed her lips and tried to swallow her feelings. It wouldn't be so bad…

Gretchen reached for a stack of letters and papers in her mailbox as she asked the school secretary, "Mary, which closet have they put my things in?"

"The one next to the cafeteria."

Gretchen nodded. "That's a pretty big space."

"You'll be sharing it with Mr. Grabel – he'll be doing individual instrument lessons in there."

Gretchen nodded slowly taking that in.

"All your supplies have already been moved in for you."

"That was nice," Gretchen mumbled without enthusiasm.

"Well, they were trying," said Mary with a chuckle.

Gretchen waved her hand full of papers in farewell as she left the office. She strolled down the hall toward the cafeteria until she reached the closet door. Opening the door, she saw boxes stacked on the shelves that lined the wall, with more boxes stacked in front of them. In front of it all, leaned two folding chairs and two music stands.

There was a knock on the open door behind her. Gretchen turned to see the long-time custodian of the school standing beside a small desk propped on a push-cart.

"Where do you want this, Mizz Parks?" he asked.

Gretchen sighed. She moved the music stands about eight feet farther back into the deep closet. She motioned to the only uncovered wall in the space. "I guess this is the only place to put it right now."

"Okay…" the custodian coughed. "won't be convenient with the door, though."

Gretchen chuckled. "Nothing is convenient, now, Lenny. It won't be until I get my things organized."

Lenny frowned. "Need some help?"

Sighing, Gretchen replied, "Not right now. I've got to think a while – figure out how to handle this."

Lenny nodded, looking relieved.

"Besides," added Gretchen, "You have more than enough to do."

"They've hired my granddaughter to help me, so it will be easier this year."

"I'm glad. You and Chip never had enough time last year."

"Yup, and I can't move as fast as I used to – not since that attack."

Gretchen smiled. She knew that, but she was glad the school wasn't forcing him out. He was so good with the kids! And the reality was that he knew so much about the workings of the school, that he would be called often by new custodians if they didn't keep him around to train them.

Lenny put the desk where Gretchen had indicated and turned his cart around. "Hope this year is a good one for you, Mizz Parks."

"Thanks, Lenny. I hope it's good for you, too."

Lenny left and Gretchen turned back to her boxes. She found the box that she had set out for the beginning of the year; it had been put on the bottom and behind several others. Just then an announcement crackled over the speaker system: "Teacher's meeting in the cafeteria now. Please, come to the cafeteria." Gretchen sighed. The organizing would have to wait. She picked up her purse and a notepad and turned to enter the cafeteria.

Back in Illinois Ben brought down his sermon notebook to work in the front room of his home so that he could be close to his mother-in-law. Ethel sat reading the paper for a while after breakfast, then she got up restlessly. She opened some drawers, looked out different windows, and moved in and out of the kitchen.

"Mother Gunther," called Ben, "is there something you need?"

Ethel stuck her head through the kitchen door. "Where's Gretchen?"

"She had to go in to work today, Mom."

"Oh…" Ethel looked a little puzzled.

"The school year is going to start soon. Gretchen had to go in to get organized."

Ethel nodded. "She's still teaching."

"Half-time, Mom. Art. She loves working with kids."

Ethel smiled. "She always did."

Ben put down his sermon. "Mom, would you like to take a walk? I know you and Gretchen have been taking walks every day."

Ethel's smile broadened. "A walk sounds good."

Ben stacked his Bible and sermon notebook on an end table next to his chair and got up. He motioned Ethel toward the door with a gallant bow. Ethel sailed out the door and stopped on the sidewalk to wait for Ben.

"I don't know where you two have been walking..." said Ben.

"Me neither," replied Ethel with a chuckle.

"Well then, we'll just take a tour of the neighborhood."

Ben held out an arm and Ethel laid her hand on it in the fashion of the gentle lady that she was. The breeze blew gently; birds sang in the trees and flew through the air. "It's a perfect temperature for a walk," declared Ben.

"It is!" agreed Ethel.

"Though, if it's perfect at nine in the morning, it will probably get hot later on."

"Yes."

"Oh, look at that cardinal. It looks so bright among the green leaves!"

"Cardinals are a bright spot."

Ben turned a corner before he continued the conversation. "I thought I'd walk you to the edge of town. It's not very far. I thought you might like to see the fields. The farmers are having a good year."

Ethel nodded and smiled as they walked along. They continued in silence until the edge of the community was reached, then they walked along the unpaved road next to the corn field. Ethel commented, "They sure plant the corn close together."

"Yes, they do," responded Ben. "It's because of the kinds of machinery they use now in farming."

"When I was growing up, we planted corn so that we could walk through it both ways."

"So you could weed it by hand?"

"Weed it by hand and pick it by hand."

"Really?" Ben was trying to figure out in his mind when corn harvesters started being used. Maybe he could check the website of that John Deere place in Moline to find out.

"Of course the big farms had more equipment than we had," continued Mom Gunther. "We just raised corn for our own use. My mother would can about 200 quarts of corn every year – that is, when all of us kids were at home – and just as many beans."

"Wow!"

"And, of course, there were preserves and kraut. And Mother canned meat when we butchered. Mostly beef and chicken."

"That sounds like a lot of work!" said Ben with feeling, even though he had heard some of this story before.

Ethel dropped her voice. "We kept this quiet so as not to embarrass Dad with the other men, but even he helped out on canning days, if there was no other work pressing."

Ben smiled.

Ethel looked over at the field of corn again. "This field is planted awfully close together."

CHAPTER 3

Back in her new space, Gretchen had boxes spread all over, even out into the hall, when the music teacher Mr. Grabel walked up.

"Oh, I'm sorry Mr. G. I've made quite a mess here!" exclaimed Gretchen. "The boxes I need to start the school year ended up on the bottom and behind everything else."

Mr. Grabel smiled. "That's typical. Don't worry; take your time. All I'm going to have in here are the chairs, music stand, and one file cabinet." He paused. "I will need to be able to set up the chairs where there is light, however."

Gretchen nodded. "Certainly. I'll be sure that I leave a space under the light open."

"Since we both just work half time in this district, Let's see if we can coordinate schedules, so that we don't get in each other's hair too much."

"Sounds, good," said Gretchen sitting down at the chair by her desk. "My understanding is that I'll basically be using this space as a store room, so I shouldn't bother you too much even on the days that I'm here."

Mr. Grabel nodded. "I'm sure it will work out fine," he assured her and walked on to the cafeteria where he sat down with some papers.

By noon Gretchen had stacked most of what she would need to start school on her desk. She was just contemplating whether to unpack the rest of her things or just stack the boxes on the storage shelves when Betsy Moth, the middle school social studies teacher came by.

"Ready for lunch?" asked Betsy.

Gretchen sighed. "I think I do need a break. I didn't bring any food with me today, though. Things are – a little different at our house right now."

Betsy laughed. "When are they not different, Gretchen?"

Gretchen shook her head, but added, "My mother has just come to stay with us."

Betsy nodded. "Well, I don't have any excuse for not bringing my lunch except that I wanted to get out of the building while I ate."

Gretchen smiled. "Where do you want to go?"

"Claire's."

"Tenderloins?"

"Tenderloins!"

"Walk or drive?" asked Gretchen.

"Let's go out and see how hot it is."

Gretchen picked up her purse and stepped out the gym door with Betsy. As they crossed to the parking lot, Gretchen noticed a girl of about 12 or 13 sitting on the curb. The girl had tan skin and frizzy light brown hair pulled back into a ponytail. She wore a simple tank top, shorts, and flip-flops.

When they got close, Betsy spoke to the child. "How goes it, Janella?"

The girl looked up revealing striking green eyes. "Oh, hi, Mrs. Moth. Keeping away from those bug zappers?"

Gretchen thought that was a strange joke, but it was obvious the girl knew her fellow teacher. She did look familiar. Those eyes… Gretchen remembered something. She remembered an odor.

Betsy Moth spoke to the girl again. "Any special reason you're here, Janella?"

Janella shrugged. "Thought school started today. My step-dad brought me and left before I realized my mistake."

Betsy nodded her head slowly. "You've been sitting here all morning?"

The girl shook her head. "You know me, Mrs. Moth. I was late, as usual."

Betsy nodded again. "Do you want to call home for a ride?"

Janella shook her head quickly. "Nope. Probably nobody home anyway. It's a nice day. I'm not bothering anyone."

Janella propped her head in her hands and stared at the ground. Gretchen and Betsy glanced at each other. Betsy held one hand like it was holding a sandwich and motioned toward her mouth, then nodded at Janella. Gretchen shrugged then nodded.

Betsy turned back to the girl. "Janella, we're walking to Claire's for lunch. Want to join us?"

Janella shrugged. "I don't want to intrude on a teacher-thing."

"I've been hoping that you and Mrs. Parks would get better acquainted," replied Betsy. "Especially with your artistic interest."

Gretchen smiled hopefully at Janella.

Janella sighed. "Yeah, it was a bummer that art for the seventh grade was first hour last year." She looked sheepishly up at Gretchen. "I didn't make it to school that early very often."

Gretchen smiled wryly. "I was wondering why I couldn't remember you as well as Mrs. Moth, but that explains it."

Betsy laid a hand on Janella's shoulder. "There is another reason that I know Janella so well," she explained. "She's one of my Talented Group kids."

"Oh?" Gretchen saw Janella make a face.

"Yes, Janella, in spite of her attendance issues, ranked very high on our standardized tests last year – but her real love is art."

Gretchen could tell that the conversation was making Janella uncomfortable. "What kind of art do you like, Janella?"

Janella shrugged again. "Cartoons, Mrs. Parks – and clay. I loved making those vases last year."

Gretchen peered at Janella thoughtfully. "You're the one whose pinch pots almost looked thrown. I remember now. You worked so hard on those vases!"

Janella looked proud, then she giggled. "And, you might remember, I made it to school on time those days."

Gretchen's left eyebrow rose, but she continued to smile. Betsy nodded knowingly. About this time they arrived at Claire's. Gretchen held the door open and Janella passed through. As the girl passed by, Gretchen caught a whiff of the smell of unwashed humanity. Gretchen's glance shifted automatically to Janella's backside. Her clothes were faded and gray. There were a few stains on the shorts of uncertain origin.

She had been a teacher too long to focus on hygiene first with her students. There were some students, though, who became identified with certain smells. The young ones who couldn't wipe well. The special ed students in diapers. The pubescent kids who were not using deodorant yet. The ones who played in the dirt in the corner of the playground had an identifiable odor also.

Gretchen realized they were now standing at the front counter. She ordered her tenderloin, a pounded and breaded pork sandwich, and put down a bill large enough to cover her tab and half of Janella's. She saw Betsy cover the rest.

Students with the odor Janella had that day were often in danger. Gretchen thought of the few other students who had had that odor of neglect or abuse. Sometimes it was hard to tell which it was. Was it a kid who didn't get clean clothes unless they did laundry themselves? Or was it a kid whose odor included the smells of old traumas?

Gretchen picked up her order and followed the other two to a table. Betsy pulled a small bottle out of her purse. "I always use a little hand sanitizer before I eat, especially if it's finger food." She squirted a little into her hand and rubbed her hands together. Then she held the bottle out to Janella and Gretchen. "Anyone else like to use this?"

Gretchen usually tried to avoid the alcohol sanitizers because they irritated her skin; however, today she reached for the bottle. After squirting some into her hand, she passed it to Janella. The conversation which took place during the meal was light, Betsy saw to that. Janella did not say that much, but wolfed down her food and then sat savoring a chocolate shake. They did not hurry to finish their meal, and they did not walk fast on the return trip to the school. Both teachers knew that letting their food digest a little before they started lifting boxes could be important.

When they got back, Betsy turned down the hall toward her room. Janella hung around the door across from Gretchen's new spot. After watching her art teacher heft a few boxes, she said, "I could help with that."

Gretchen unbent and smiled at Janella. "I just might let you do that."

Janella left her post by the door and approached the closet. Inside the enclosed space her odor was more potent. Gretchen made up her mind to ignore it.

"Let's see..." Gretchen looked over the boxes on the floor. "I think I'll have you help me unpack this paper. I'll arrange it on the top shelf so I can see it, but have it safe from damage." She pulled a small cutter out of her desk and broke the seals on a couple of boxes. "You hand me the bundles of paper, and I'll arrange it, so I know where it is."

"Okay." Janella opened the first box which was filled with 12x18 white paper. She handed fifty sheet packages up to Gretchen who arranged it in two stacks against the wall on the top shelf.

When that box was empty, Gretchen stretched her arms and bent her back. "I'm glad you are helping. This paper gets heavy fast."

Janella chuckled. "No problem. I was getting tired of sitting on that curb."

"Well, you really are a help. Let's try the colored paper now."

Gretchen and Janella worked for a solid hour unpacking supplies that would be used in the art program fairly soon. Other boxes they stuck at the back of the deep shelves out of the way.

"What do you want done with the clay boxes?" Janella asked, kicking one with her foot. It didn't budge.

Gretchen giggled. "I'm not going to ask you to lift them, if that's what you're thinking."

Janella sighed in relief. "I was wondering if I could."

"We'll shove these under the shelves. No lifting required."

"Good!" Janella got down on her hands and knees to get a good push on the boxes.

Gretchen knew how to use the heel of her shoe to get the leverage she needed.

"What are you going to do when it's time to use this stuff?" asked Janella.

"I open it up and take one sack out at a time," replied Gretchen. "That way I'm just dealing with half the weight."

Janella nodded knowingly. "Good idea, but I've had another one. Putting that stuff way back under there can lead to mold growin'."

Gretchen laughed. "You're right! Sometimes I need to take allergy meds when we start doing clay here at school. Still, some experts say that a little mold actually improves the clay."

"No!"

Gretchen nodded. "Yes. But I will tell you that the clay is wrapped in plastic bags. That minimizes mold growth."

Janella just shook her head. "I'm learning things about being an art teacher that I wouldn't have guessed – ever."

Just then a buzzer rang. "What time is it?" asked Janella, as Gretchen glanced at her watch. Gretchen turned the watch to face Janella. "Oh, I'd better get outside. My stepdad may be coming anytime."

Gretchen nodded. "Thanks for your help, Janella."

"You're welcome, Mrs. Parks." Janella gave a little wave as she turned to go.

Gretchen switched to organizing her desk. As she sat there, she glanced up several times and saw that Janella had returned to her spot on the curb. The desk was put into order, she'd plugged in her computer and checked her email; and she'd found her template for lesson plans. Also opening up the calendar of last year's projects, and her scope and sequence, she spread out the packing slip from her order. With all that in front of her, Gretchen started making notes for her upcoming lesson plans. It didn't take long for her to get to the point that she wanted a chance to move and think, rather than sit at her desk.

As she left her "office" Gretchen noticed two things. First, she noticed that the air seemed fresher out in the hall. Second, she noticed Janella still sitting on the curb. She walked down the hall, ducked into the women's restroom, and then stopped by the soda machine. Needing a little pick-me-up, Gretchen got a caffeinated drink. She popped the top of the beverage can and started drinking as she returned to her room. Passing a doorway, which was propped open because the air conditioning was not on, she saw a rather nice van pull up next to Janella. Janella was standing by the time the van stopped and she opened the door. Gretchen couldn't see who was driving, but it was obvious that the girl knew whoever it was.

Later, as Gretchen Parks drove home, she thought about the smart, helpful girl who smelled. The girl who was willing to sit all day on a curb rather than call her stepdad to come get her. The girl who looked sad, even when she smiled. "Dear Lord, help that girl! And, if I am supposed to be part of that help, let me be aware of what I need to do."

She parked the car, and walked toward her home, wondering how Ben and her mother had made it through the day.

CHAPTER 4

"Hi, Honey. I'm home!" Gretchen closed the door behind herself as she heard a noise in the direction of the kitchen.

Ben peeked through the kitchen door. "We're in here, Gretchen, having a snack."

"That sounds good. What are you having?"

Ben chuckled. "Just bread and jelly and a glass of milk."

Gretchen smiled as she walked to the kitchen, detouring to put her school bag at the bottom of the stairs. Bread and jelly. That had often been her snack when she got home from school as a child. It brought back memories. She hugged Ben and then her mom while saying, "I remember coming home from school when I was little. Mom, you would have a plate on the table containing bread spread with jelly, and a cold glass of milk standing next to it."

Gretchen's mom continued, "And in the winter, hot chocolate."

Gretchen nodded and closed her eyes, savoring that first sweet bite. "What a nice surprise!"

"Glad you like it, honey," replied Ben. "It was your Mom's idea."

"Thanks, Mom."

"Ben told me you were at school," replied Ethel.

Gretchen frowned.

Ben chuckled. "I told Mom Gunther that at least five times today."

Gretchen was remembering that she also had told her mother where she was going. It was obvious once again that her short-term memory was damaged. What problems could that cause?

Ethel replied, "I just couldn't accept that my girl had never graduated from school."

Ben let out a loud guffaw. Evan Gretchen chuckled. This was another reminder her mom's memory might be broken, but not her sense of humor.

The next day was supposed to be a repeat of the last, and it started out that way. Gretchen ate breakfast with her mother. As she went out the door, Ben stood next to Ethel; both made a point of mentioning that Gretchen was going to her school. Gretchen went to teachers meetings soon after she got to school, sitting next to her friend Betsy Moth.

At home, Ben and Ethel took a walk. Then Ethel sat down with one of her notebooks, and Ben sat down with his Bible and sermon materials. Ben found it harder to concentrate sitting on the sofa than at his office desk. He got up to stretch and get a glass of water. Ethel was nodding in the chair next to her bed; her pencil and notebook on the floor beside her. Ben got his water, set it on the small table next to his seat, and soon was napping himself.

Back at the staff meeting, Betsy Moth slapped her thigh over her pants pocket. She stretched to one side and slipped her cell phone out of that pocket. Bringing it up to reading level, she looked briefly at it, then got up and hurried out the back of the room. Gretchen glanced back a minute later and saw Betsy putting away her phone and moving toward the school superintendent. He was standing at the back of the room listening to Principal Mitchell explain room and scheduling changes for the year. A few minutes later, Gretchen's phone vibrated and she glanced down to see a message from Betsy: *Home emergency. Take 2 of any papers they pass out.*

Gretchen did as her friend asked and delivered the duplicates to Betsy's room after the meeting was over. Then she turned to go to her closet. As she passed an open door, she saw someone sitting on the parking lot curb. She paused for a closer look. It was Janella. Gretchen stopped completely. Should she invite Janella in to help her again? She had decision-making work today. Janella couldn't help with that. Gretchen continued on to her room.

A little later the phone just inside the cafeteria door started to ring. Gretchen peeked out of her area and into the cafeteria. No one else was around, so she walked over and answered the phone. "Hello?"

"Gretchen?"

"Yes."

"It's Mary in the office."

"Hi, Mary. What can I do for you?"

"It's what I can do for you – maybe. Some of us were going to order lunch in and wondered if you would be interested."

"I just might be."

"We were going to get pizza from the Corner Garage."

"Sounds good. Put me down for one..." Gretchen thought about Janella sitting outside. "No, make that three slices."

"Three? You must be hungry!"

"Have you noticed a student sitting outside?"

"Janella?"

"Yes."

"Wasn't she out there yesterday?"

"Uh-huh. Betsy and I took her to lunch yesterday with us. Said she forgot that it was just a work day and that no one would be home to get her until later."

"Oh."

"Apparently she didn't tell her family that today was a work day too."

"Hmm. Would rather sit in the parking lot all day than be at home."

Gretchen was quiet for a moment. "Anyway, the other two slices are for her."

"Okay. I need to stretch my legs a little, so I'll be down to collect your money soon."

It wasn't long before Gretchen heard high heels clicking rapidly down the hallway. She reached for her purse and fished around in it for the amount of money needed to pay for her part of the pizza order.

She had just finished zipping up her handbag, when Mary stuck her head around the door of the closet. "Gretchen, I think you are needed at home."

"Oh?"

"Ben called. He says that he's lost your mother."

"My mother? What?" Gretchen couldn't believe what she

was hearing.

"Your mother." Mary took a breath. "Ben said that they had both been dozing in the living room. When he woke up, your mom was gone!"

"Oh, dear! I thought you were coming after the pizza money." Gretchen stretched out her hand. "Here it is."

Mary took it, but shook her head. "You don't need to pay me. You need to get home."

Gretchen waved Mary off from returning the money. "Just see that Janella gets her share." She looked around, collecting her thoughts.

"Need anything?" asked Mary.

Gretchen grimaced. "Just a new head… and apparently alarms on the doors out of my house."

The screen door banged closed as Ben ran out to meet Gretchen at the curb. The expression on his face shifted from guilt to worry as he spoke. "I'm so glad you are home, and so sorry that this happened!"

Gretchen hugged her husband in greeting as she asked, "What happened exactly."

"Well, it's harder to stay alert on the couch than in my office chair. I noticed your mom was dozing, so I didn't try too hard to stay awake. But when I opened my eyes later, Mom Gunther was gone!"

"How long ago did this happen?"

Ben rubbed his forehead. "Let's see… it's about noon now… It's been about an hour and a half… maybe a little longer."

Gretchen's mouth must have dropped open, because Ben hurried on in his explanation. "At first I thought she was in the bathroom. Then I checked upstairs. Then outside. I was so sure she would be some place close… some place obvious… that I didn't think about calling you at first." He glanced sheepishly at her. "Then I didn't want to call you."

"Have you called the sheriff?"

"Right before I called the school." He looked at her sheepishly again. "I was so flustered that I pushed the wrong button on my speed dial and called the school office rather than your cell."

Gretchen waved her hand in dismissal. "Mary needed to know anyway. What do we do now?"

"The sheriff said that someone needs to stay home, in case Ethel finds her way home – or is brought home. Now that you're here, could you stay? I'll go out and retrace the route of the walk we took this morning."

Gretchen nodded.

"You can look for any clues I might have missed."

"I don't know what that would be, but I'll look."

Ben bade her a hasty goodbye and jumped in the car. Then, in contrast to his initial haste, he took off slowly, looking back and forth around every house he drove past.

Gretchen took a tour of their yard before going inside, but saw nothing out of the ordinary. She looked at the back yards up and down their block. No fences, indicated an informal and friendly relationship between neighbors. She sighed. Today she wondered if a fence would have helped her mother stay closer to home.

Going inside, she found herself looking in closets and under beds. Hoping, and yet not hoping, that she would find her mother hiding in some corner. Ben returned briefly, told Gretchen that he had found nothing on his swing around their walk route, and said that he was going back to the cornfield. Behind it was an alfalfa field where a farmer was cutting hay for feed. "I'm going to ask the farmer to watch out for a lost lady as he works."

Gretchen winced as her over-active imagination pictured her mother being bailed.

As Ben left again, she sat down in the chair her mother had been using beside her bed. On the floor to one side was one of her mother's notebooks. Gretchen picked it up. Her mom's journal. Would it contain any clues? It had been folded open. Glancing briefly at the entry on the page in front of her, she realized that it had been made a few days after her father had died.

Today I think the reality of Herman's passing is taking hold.

I have been in shock in some ways through all this process. What do I feel? Grief, yes. But I have been grieving a long time. Fear, yes. I do not know how I am going to go on alone, though in some ways I have been alone for a long time. But, you know, I don't feel alone. I feel God's presence today. That may be why I can also accept the reality of Herm's death. So I also have hope. Ha! And then I feel guilty about feeling hopeful. I'm a mess! But that's nothing new and I've survived. Today I will just hold on. I will let myself feel a little crazy. I will let myself feel both sad and hopeful. I will take some time to walk, to take care of myself. To do some of those small tasks that I have been letting go.

Gretchen wondered if reading about taking a walk had somehow influenced her mom. She shook her head. No way to tell. She turned back to the beginning of the notebook.

Inside the cover Gretchen found the following:

Hi, Friend or Family Member,
This book is for you as well as for me. My doctor told me to start writing a journal every day. I think it was as a kind of therapy, but I've thought of another reason for it. In the future you may have questions that I can't remember the answers to. I want to write down the answers now, as I am living them, so that you can have them later.
Hope what you read here is helpful for you. (And I also hope the therapy the doctor ordered works!)
Love, Ethel Louise Gunther

Gretchen found tears coming to her eyes. Were there any clues in here as to her mother's whereabouts today? Gretchen doubted it. But there could be clues as to what her mother had been dealing with in the last few years. Because she couldn't think of anything else to do, she read a little further.

One more thing before I start the journal in earnest – If you are wondering what I would want you to know if I could only communicate one thing to you, here it is. If you want to be more than a flower that blooms and fades, or a bit of dust landing on this earth for a few years, seek a relationship with God.

The one who created us knows us even more than we know ourselves. He is the one who will never change or leave us. He is the one who always knows the truth, even when everything around us seems false or confusing. I can't explain it very well, but seeking Him is a better use of your time than finding a mate, raising your children, or having a successful career.

If you consider this the ramblings of a fragile old woman (which it is), then I ask that you just remember what I have said when everything goes wrong.

The screen door screeched and a sound of happy voices entered the house. Gretchen recognized her mother's voice and the other was familiar also. She hurriedly closed the notebook and put it inside the bedside stand.

"Mom?" Gretchen called as she stood up.

"Yes, girl." Ethel Gunther responded as she and neighbor Dorine Carmine entered the room.

"Hello, Mrs. Parks," Mrs. Carmine said.

"Hello. Mrs. – ah – what –where --?"

"Oh! Have you been looking for Ethel?"

"Well, ah, yes."

"Oh my! I thought Ethel was home alone!"

"You did?"

"Yes, Ethel saw me working in my backyard and came over to talk. We went in for some coffee, then I invited her to stay for lunch."

Gretchen collapsed back into the chair.

Mrs. Carmine looked a little worried, but said, "We had such a nice visit! You know I get a little lonely sometimes. It was so nice to have company that I guess I didn't think about whether we should check back here sooner."

Now Gretchen felt guilty. She had been passing Mrs. Carmine's almost every day for years, but had only been inside her house a few times. She should have been a better neighbor. Then another thought entered her mind. "I've got to call Ben!"

That evening Gretchen and Ben were not quite so comfortable leaving Mom Gunther downstairs when they went upstairs to get ready for bed.

"She hasn't had a problem in the night in all the time we've had her here." Ben said this as if he was trying to convince himself.

"We've got the signs to guide her to the bathroom," added Gretchen. "And we've left the light on over the kitchen sink for a nightlight."

Ben plopped himself down on the bed. "I'm so glad that you're not working tomorrow." He sighed heavily. "And I'm glad that Mrs. Carmine said that she would enjoy regular visits from Mom Gunther."

Gretchen ran her fingers through her hair. "That should help in the short term, but..." She sighed too. "We haven't even moved things out of her apartment in Kansas City, and I'm wondering if Mom will need to be put into one of those homes," After a pause, she continued in a voice not much more than a whisper, "for her own safety..."

The phone rang by the bedside. Ben leaned over, looked at the caller ID, then picked it up, passing it directly to Gretchen. "Hello?" said Gretchen as she wondered who could be calling that late at night.

"Gretchen? This is Betsy Moth."

"Yes, Betsy. It's me."

"Gretchen, I'm sorry to be calling so late, but I figured early on your day off wouldn't be any better."

"What's wrong, Betsy?"

"Oh, what's not wrong!" declared Betsy, then she caught herself. "I'm sorry. Lots of things are right, but at the moment it's hard to remember them. You see, my husband is very sick..."

"What is it?"

There was a brief pause, then Betsy answered, "The doctors are working on that. All I can say right now is that this has been coming on for a while and – and now it's got to the point that I had to take him to the hospital today. That's what that call was about at school."

"Oh, Betsy! I'm sorry."

Betsy sighed audibly. "Well, it's just a part of life."

"Yet man is born unto trouble as the sparks fly upward," quoted Gretchen from Job 5:7.

Betsy chuckled. "I should have known you'd have a Bible verse for the situation." In spite of the chuckle, her last words had sounded more like a sob. She cleared her throat. "Anyway, I've just gotten off the phone with our principal and he's arranging a sub for me for the first few days of school. That will take care of my regular classes, but I have a favor to ask of you. You are the only one in the school that has any experience with the problem solving challenge."

"I don't know that much, Betsy. My son was just in the program when he was in junior high and high school."

"That's six more years of experience than anyone else has, Gretchen. Mr. Mitchell has said that he has the okay to increase your time two hours per week, if you would help with the program this year. I will help when I can, but I told him I would need someone who could be there on a regular basis for the times I might not be able to."

"Oh." Gretchen was not sure what to say.

"I know you have two full days of work when you come, but Mr. Mitchell said that he'd work with you to arrange your hours however was best for you – one full day and two five-hour days – or whatever."

"Betsy, I want to help, but I'm not sure I should answer without thinking about it."

"I know, Gretchen, and praying about it."

"Yes," Gretchen responded weakly.

"Our principal will be talking to you tomorrow, but gave me permission to call you tonight so that you could be thinking about it." Here Betsy paused, but Gretchen waited silently. "Gretchen, Janella is on the problem challenge team."

"Oh."

"Yes. That's another reason I thought about you as a helper. Not everyone can – uh – put up with Janella."

Gretchen found herself nodding, even though Betsy couldn't see her. "I think I understand what you mean."

"I knew you would. She's had so many difficult things to face in her young life – so many people she has lost – I want to keep some sense of continuity for her at school, and – and this program has been good for her."

"I will think and pray about this, Betsy. Don't worry about it. Mr. Mitchell and I will be sure something is worked out."

"Oh, thank you, Gretchen! You are a jewel!" Betsy's voice caught on the last word. She cleared her voice again. "And Gretchen –"

"Yes."

"Pray for me, too. It's – it's harder sometimes to handle when your husband is sick than if –"

"Than if you were sick yourself," finished Gretchen.

Later that night, Gretchen lay awake, thinking about the phone call, the earlier events of the day, and her last words with Ben after Betsy had hung up.

"Maybe this will be a blessing," Ben had said. "The school will let you alter your schedule in a way that might help with our situation. And with our extra expenses now, the money won't hurt."

When Gretchen mentioned that Betsy had seemed to avoid naming her husband's illness, Ben mused, "Either it's some delicate area – like the prostate – or (and more likely) it's a mental or emotional problem. People are still more reserved about sharing that information."

Gretchen thought he was probably right. She knew that last year Betsy had left as quickly as she could after school each day. What she continued to wonder about was whether it was something like a mental breakdown, or some kind of dementia or brain injury. *Oh well, I don't need to know,* thought Gretchen. *What I need to do is ask God to help.* And she did, which helped her to drift off to sleep.

The next morning Gretchen got a call shortly after 8:00 a.m. from her principal. Half an hour later, several decisions had been made. Gretchen would work Tuesdays and Thursdays from 11:00 to 4:00 p.m. and all day on Friday which was Ben's day off. She would take a break from her art cart to meet with the problem solving challenge teams during study halls and after school on those two days. Gretchen's mom would stay with their neighbor on Tuesdays and Thursdays from the time Gretchen left until Ben came home at noon. All that decided, Gretchen turned her attention first to her husband, and, after he left, to her mother.

They ate breakfast again together, took a walk together, and had almost the same conversation that day that they had every day during their walks.

Ethel Gunther saw the corn field and said, "They plant that corn awfully close together."

"Yes, they do, Mom," replied Gretchen. "It's because of the kind of machinery they use today on the farms."

"We planted it so that we could walk through it both ways, so we could walk the corn and weed it by hand."

"That makes sense."

After the walk, mother and daughter worked together on laundry and then lunch. Then they settled down in their favorite chairs. Ethel got out two of her notebooks and a pencil. She opened one and then the other, flipping through the pages until she found a blank one. The other one she held out toward Gretchen.

"Gretchen, this one is for you."

Gretchen got up and reached over for the notebook. "You want me to read it?"

Ethel nodded. "If you don't have something else you've got to do."

"Well, I don't right now... so I will read a little."

Gretchen settled herself back into the chair. This was the same volume she had opened the other day. She recognized the inscription inside the cover. She opened it from the back for some reason and flipped several pages until something caught her eye. She started to read.

My neighbor Mrs. Gloria Velasquez said that I should consider putting my husband away. I couldn't do that anymore than I could let her take me to the hospital. I slipped and fell in the bathroom today while I was cleaning. Hit my head on the edge of the tub and was knocked out cold. When Gloria came over and knocked on the door, Herman answered. She asked where I was and he said, "She locked herself in the bathroom, 'cause she's mad at me."

Mrs. V. thought that sounded strange, so she went to the bathroom door. It was not locked, in fact it was open a crack. Gloria pushed it open more and found me on the floor, still out. She wanted to take me to the hospital, but I couldn't leave Herm. He hadn't done anything wrong; he just doesn't understand. But my head hurts like everything! I may end up going to the hospital tomorrow if it's not any better.

Gretchen thoughtfully glanced over at her mom who was peacefully napping in her chair. She had never realized what her mother had gone through. Her dad had reached a point when he couldn't even get help in an emergency; he could not understand what the emergency was. And her mom – she wondered if the dementia was related to that concussion. *What if Mom had gone to the hospital? Could they have done anything to keep this from happening?* Gretchen shook her head. It did no good to think about that now. The doctors had indicated there was permanent damage. They might be able to minimize further damage with medication, but what was done was done. *At least the damage had not affected her personality. Mom was still her sweet self – just limited.* The nurse had whispered that a little further to the front and it could have been much worse.

Gretchen shook her head to clear her thoughts and turned back to her reading.

We had a visit from the police this evening. I was in the kitchen cooking supper when I heard the front door open and close. Since I hadn't heard the bell, I went to check. Herm wasn't in the living room watching television, like I'd left him. I looked outside. At first I couldn't figure out what he was doing, standing at our second floor railing, fumbling with something in front of him; then I saw the narrow stream of liquid.

Quickly I opened the door and spoke Herm's name. He half turned – enough to confirm that he somehow thought he was in the bathroom. I said, "Herm, zip up your pants and come back inside." Somewhere in the background I heard someone yelling something; I didn't really hear what, but yelled out "Sorry, he's got dementia" as I took Herm back in. I took him into the kitchen with me as I finished up supper.

It was just as we were sitting down to supper that the doorbell rang. The officer waiting outside was very nice. He told us that someone had reported what Herm had done and he had to check it out. I explained the situation, while Herm sat there, apparently not comprehending the conversation. The officer said that he strongly recommended me looking into a care facility for Herm. When I blurted out, "No!" he asked if money was a problem and mentioned a county-supported facility. I swallowed hard and told him I would look into it. I don't think he believed me, because he said that he'd check back with us in a couple of days to see how we were doing.

Gretchen looked up as her mother stirred. Ethel smiled across the room at her daughter and pushed herself out of the soft chair. Gretchen started to get up herself, but Ethel shook her head and said one word, "bathroom." Gretchen pointed. Ethel nodded and turned in the right direction. Gretchen heard the bathroom door close and returned to her reading. She started at the top of the next entry.

I got Gloria Velasquez to watch Herm today. I visited the two closest "homes" advertising they had memory care. Both seemed nice, but awfully expensive. Their administrators gave me lots of papers about finances, contracts, etc. Now I have to study them and figure out what is truly best. God help me! No cooking today. Sandwiches for lunch and I'm going to have Chinese delivered for supper.

The sound of the toilet flushing reached Gretchen. She closed up the notebook and checked her watch. It was time to fix lunch.

CHAPTER 5

The plans that they had made became the routine of life. Ben kept regular office hours. Gretchen started her art classes and the problem solving groups. Ethel seemed to settle in and started to recognize her way around the house. Neighbor Mrs. Carmine did really seem to enjoy the idea of having Ethel over several times a week.

Labor Day came quickly and Gretchen drove a borrowed van to Kansas City to clean out her mom's apartment. Neighbor Sylvia came over to help. One thing surprised Gretchen. Many things were already in boxes.

Turning to Sylvia, Gretchen scratched her head. "I thought Mom just expected to come for a few days visit. Did you do this packing?"

Sylvia shook her head. "Not me."

"Hmm. And these boxes are so well labeled! That's not what I'd expect of someone with Mom's problems."

"Mrs. Parks –"

"Gretchen."

Sylvia smiled. "Mrs. – Gretchen. It's just been the last few months that your mom has gotten more confused. I moved in shortly after her husband – your dad's – death and she seemed perfectly fine. Grieving, yes. Confused – no."

Gretchen acknowledged this information with a nod.

"I notice that a lot of the boxes indicate dates – and that they contain stuff like my older sister put away when she started having kids."

"Hmm… yes. And some of it is Dad's stuff."

"I wonder –"

"If Mom packed up stuff to get them out of Dad's way."

"Or to protect the stuff from someone who wasn't thinking

clearly."

Gretchen took a deep breath as she remembered what she had read in her mom's journal.

"I know something else," Sylvia continued. "Your Mom donated a lot of stuff to the Salvation Army. Their bus came by to pick up things more than once."

Gretchen's eyebrows rose. "Well... I may not have expected this, but it should make my job easier." Sylvia stacked boxes in the living room while Gretchen sorted out what was in drawers. She packed clothes in suitcases and garment bags, piling things that were in disrepair or of questionable use in a pile.

Turning to Sylvia, she asked, "Is there anything in the apartment you would like?"

"Uh – I don't – Uh..."

Gretchen could tell that her question had made Sylvia uncomfortable. "Let me be more specific," she explained. "Mom isn't going to need most of her kitchen things. And, besides a favorite chair and her dresser, she's not going to need most of her furniture."

"You could store it."

Gretchen sighed. "For what? Why don't I sort out what I plan on taking and then you will know what you have first pick of."

"Why don't I go get us some lunch while you do that?"

Gretchen grabbed her purse and pressed a bill into Sylvia's hand. "You've been so much help! At least let me pay for the meal."

Sylvia saluted with the hand holding the money and left.

While she was gone, Gretchen unloaded the kitchen shelves and cupboards. She found a few items that her mother might have sentimental thoughts about: an old cast iron cornbread pan, an ancient flower sifter, an old cookbook with notations in the margins, and a few hand-stitched dishtowels. She put those in a box, labeled it, and stacked it with the others in the living room. Everything else she left out to pack in more boxes to be given to someone.

She found some blue painter's tape and wrote *KEEP* on a piece. Then she stuck it on her mom's favorite chair. She put another on a little magazine rack that she knew her father had made when she was a child. There was also a dresser that had been inherited from Gretchen's great-grandmother; it got a taped message also. In the bathroom, Gretchen placed toiletries and medications in a soft-sided bag, throwing out anything that was outdated or broken. She was just deciding whether the shiny bathtub needed a final cleansing when she heard Sylvia returning.

As she set out several cardboard containers and the aroma of Chinese food filled the room, Sylvia asked, "Did I make it back before you reached the bathroom?"

"I've cleaned out the drawers and cabinet, but that's all." Gretchen answered.

"Good! I came over here a few days ago and cleaned everything I could get to without messing with Mrs. Gunther's stuff."

"Bless you!" declared Gretchen. "Mom did have a jewel for a neighbor!"

"Well, I think you've got that backwards," remarked Sylvia. "When I was moving in the lady who had lived here before gave me orders. 'Be nice to your neighbor,' she told me. 'That lady is a sweetheart – and she's just lost her husband.'"

Gretchen looked thoughtful. "I was reading about her former neighbor just the other day."

"In Ethel's journals."

"Have you read them?"

"No, though she told me I could if I wanted to. I figured they were more for family."

"I think she considered you her Kansas City family."

Sylvia smiled and picked up her plastic fork. Then she put it back down and folded her hands. Gretchen smiled and folded her own.

"Do you want to pray or do I?" asked Sylvia.

"Whichever you prefer."

"Okay. I don't always remember, but here in Ethel's apartment, it somehow would seem terrible not to pray." Sylvia bowed her head and said a grace that sounded much like Gretchen remembering her mother's.

By the end of the day, Gretchen had packed the borrowed van with boxes, her mother's favorite chair, and the dresser which she knew had been made by a great-grandfather. She knew that her job had been made much easier by the fact that her parents had moved from the family farm and done their own sorting about five years before her father's death. It had also been easier because her mother had put so much in boxes, though she still wasn't sure why. And then there had been Sylvia's help.

Most of the furniture and household goods left in a Salvation Army Thrift Store truck, though she had given Sylvia the kitchen table and chairs, and an old beat-up chest of drawers which had set in the back hallway at the farm. Gretchen didn't understand why her parents had saved that chest when they moved, and she didn't understand why Sylvia would have been interested in taking it when she refused other nicer pieces. Sylvia's comment when saying she would like it was this. "It's got character, like your parents."

As she sat on her mother's mattress on the floor of the empty apartment that night, she called Ben at home.

"How's it going, honey?" asked Ben.

"Better than I thought it would. Mom had lots of things in boxes already."

"Wow. That's nice."

"Yes, and Sylvia has been helping."

"She's a jewel. Hope you gave her something."

"She wouldn't take money, but I gave her the kitchen table and an old chest."

"Good."

"Also paid for her meals – though she went to get them for us."

"Certainly."

Gretchen paused, slumping as she did so.

"Tired?" Ben couldn't see her, but he knew his wife.

Gretchen chuckled. "Exhausted."

"Do you have a comfortable bed for the night?"

"I have Mom's mattress and bedding on the floor. Can't sell it and I think we can squeeze it in the van."

"Sounds like a good idea. Your mom may be more comfortable on her own mattress than on Calvin's old one."

"Sylvia's going to take me to church in the morning before I leave."

"Good. We'll miss you, but I'm glad you won't miss worship."

"Me too." Gretchen paused a moment then continued. "How are you and Mom doing?"

"Very well. She's asked several times where you are, but has seemed to adjust to me and our neighbor staying with her."

"I'm glad. Tell her I love her."

"I will. And I'll tell her you will probably be home tomorrow."

"Yes!"

"But, Gretchen, stop if you get tired."

"I know."

"Good. I love you."

"I love you."

The next morning, Gretchen dressed in a clean pair of slacks and shirt, hoping that Sylvia would take her to a church where casual dress was permissible. She got out a granola bar for her breakfast, but heard her phone's call tone from where it lay on the floor by the mattress she'd slept on.

"Gretchen?" It was Sylvia's voice. "I've got scrambled eggs and toast over here. Come join me."

"That sounds great!"

"I knew you'd given away the fridge."

They ate together, then Sylvia asked, "Do you want to go to your Mom's church or mine?"

"Well –" Gretchen tried to figure out what to say in response.

"Your mom got me started going back to church by inviting me to hers, but it's – well – it was mostly older folks."

Gretchen nodded.

"My church is within walking distance – just a couple of blocks – and it has a nine o'clock service."

"I'd like to visit your church," said Gretchen.

The church turned out to be in a former store. The front
display window was now an over-sized diorama of Jesus
welcoming the children, made with old mannequins and large
dolls. Stuck to the window itself was a printed paper with
service times and office hours on it. Standing in front of the
church were a couple holding what looked like lunch sacks. As
Gretchen and Sylvia approached the church, they saw two
street people approach the couple and take a bag. One turned
and went inside with his bag. The other scurried off, already
eating the sandwich it had contained.

Sylvia turned to Gretchen. "We don't require anyone to
attend services to get food, but there are drinks inside and more
to take with them after the service."

Gretchen nodded. She had never been to a church that not
only ministered to homeless people, but actively sought them
to attend their services. "How did you decide on this church?"
she asked.

"There was construction in front of our apartments, so I had
to find another way to get to work. It was a Wednesday about
eleven in the morning. Brother Manuel was standing just where
you see that couple today. He was handing out apples and
hotdogs."

By then they had reached the church. The couple outside
offered them a bag, but Sylvia shook her head and responded,
"We're good." Entering the building, Gretchen saw a collection
of chairs facing a black metal music stand on the left side of
the room. The front row and the back row were old couches
and stuffed chairs, while the middle rows looked like the
folding metal chairs Ben had finally gotten the trustees of his
church to give away last summer. Beyond the rows of chairs,
several tables were set up in front of an old fountain counter on
one side, with a walled-in area, windows running the length of
the wall, forming what had to be a children's area by the plastic
toys visible inside.

Several people sat eating at the tables. The smell of coffee
filled the place. A young woman sat with a keyboard on her
knees playing old hymns. A couple of people about retirement
age, and a couple of apparent street people, stood around her

singing along. There were two young couples with children and several college students, but at least half of the people in the room looked like they could use a bath.

Sylvia spoke to several people, introduced Gretchen, and led her to some chairs. When Gretchen looked askance at the old metal ones, a young man clutching a paper sack gallantly got up out of his faded arm chair and pushed it up to the row where they stood, motioning for Gretchen to sit. She flushed, thanked him, and sat down.

The music changed from old hymns to simple choruses as the service started. The sermon was an interesting combination of doctoral thesis and children's object lessons. Both the college group and the street people clapped and yelled out comments, as the Spirit moved them. The sermon closed with a challenge to stay for the post-service discussion. The service ended with the singing of "Just as I Am," the song that had closed Billy Graham's crusades.

Gretchen realized that there had been no offering and looked around for a way to make a donation. Sylvia must have realized what she was looking for because she put one hand on Gretchen's arm and pointed toward a table-high metal urn with a hole in the top. Gretchen had never seen an offering container like it, but then she'd never been in a church service like it either. She liked it; it seemed real.

That night at home, as she struggled to stay awake long enough to cover her trip's highlights, she heard Ben respond to her description of the service with this comment; "I wonder if the pastor ever has jobs for service mission groups."

As Gretchen slipped into dreamland, she smiled. She hoped that Sylvia and that storefront church would have some future connection to their lives.

CHAPTER 6

Gretchen was glad that she didn't have to go in to school on Monday. It had been a long weekend and she needed a day to re-adjust. After breakfast, she and her mother took their regular walk. They greeted Dorine Carmine, talked about the how the corn was planted, and watched the birds.

Even though Gretchen wondered if her mother would remember, she explained about how Sylvia had helped with the packing and sorting. Ethel nodded appreciatively and told a couple stories of her own about her helpful neighbor. Gretchen described what she had brought with her, and told her that they could start unpacking the trailer later that morning.

"Did you bring the dresser?" asked Ethel.

"Of course, Mom."

"Good," Ethel said, then changed the subject back to the birds.

Ben came home for lunch, then stayed long enough to take a few boxes up to the attic. Next he drove to a restaurant close to SouthPark Mall in the Quad Cities for a meeting of the QCUMG, the Quad Cities United Mission Group. He walked into the restaurant's meeting room and looked for an empty spot around the table. There was one by the Hoovers, the pastoral couple of a small church in Silvis. He nodded as he sat down, but didn't say anything, because the chairman of the group had already started speaking.

"We've united to try to provide opportunities of Christian service for ourselves and our church members," Chairman Buchanan said, after his opening prayer. "We're small congregations. Not mega-churches who can organize their own multiple mission trips each year. So, we're looking for opportunities to serve, by working together."

Several people made suggestions. Then one of the most conservative members spoke. "We shouldn't plan any projects that we can't all agree on. The success of what we do should be measured by how many people come to Jesus."

There was some uncomfortable shifting in chairs.

Ben cleared his throat and raised his hand. The chairman nodded in his direction. "I hear what Brother Martin is saying, and in many ways I agree with him. However, whenever short-term help comes to a mission field, they may or may not be in a position to directly witness. Sometimes there is a language barrier. Sometimes, what needs to be done is a support ministry, so that the long-term people are more effective soul-winners."

A minister's wife, who belonged to one of the most liberal churches represented at the table, was the next to speak. "Even Jesus did things for people, besides save their souls. He healed people, talked to people. Sometimes, at the moment, the most important thing we can do for someone is just show we care."

Mrs. Hoover waved her hand. "I've heard that it often takes a series of exposures to Christianity before someone is ready to make a decision. We may be the first or second time someone meets a loving Christian. Do we negate the importance of that?"

Chairman Buchanan took charge again. "There are over twenty churches represented here. We could really get bogged down if we had to come to theological consensus about every mission opportunity. May I suggest that whoever brings a project to the group brings a belief statement and mission statement – or something like that – from the group we would be working with. No one would be forced to serve on any project, so if the type of service or the receiving organization did not meet with a member's approval, they could just opt out. If all except one opts out, then it would be up to the presenting church whether they take on the project alone."

All was quiet for a moment, then the conservative preacher again spoke. "A Solomon-like statement. I still have some reservations, but what you said is true about how easily we could get bogged down. I do not want us to be stopped before we get started."

Everyone else also approved Rev. Buchanan's statement. Ben didn't say anything about Gretchen's experience over the weekend. He figured he could get more information, including a statement of faith, from the Kansas City mission church before the next meeting.

Ben found himself praying for the group on his way home, and later with Gretchen before they went to sleep that night.

The days fell into a predictable pattern. Gretchen and Ben's work schedules were set. Mother Gunther looked forward to her visits with their neighbor. Church activities returned to the fall schedule, but most meetings took place in the evening. Gretchen was not as active as she had been in the last few years, because she again had someone at home to watch over.

Gretchen brought home work from her art classes and the problem solving groups, so she didn't have to be gone any more than necessary. The art classes began design principle lessons, and Gretchen used a variation on lessons she had taught before to streamline her planning process. The problem solvers were studying the purpose and future of toys. Gretchen encouraged them to bring a favorite toy from their younger childhood and one they liked right now. The high interest of the students helped them stay on the task of studying toys, in spite of Gretchen's limited experience.

Ben scheduled as many individual meetings as he could in the mornings and over lunch time. His posted office hours were from 8:30 a.m. to 12:30 p.m. If he had people he needed to talk to in the afternoons, he did it by phone. Occasionally both Gretchen and Ethel would both go to the church with Ben to chaperon him while he had counseling sessions – especially if they were with women.

One afternoon Gretchen found herself distracted by an itchy red spot on her arm as she sat with the eighth grade problem solving team. There had been some chatter about a game brought in by one of the students. Finally, Gretchen broke into the conversation. "We've had lots of fun studying this topic."

The kids nodded.

"It's time we think about some of the problems associated

with toys."

Anthony wiggled his fingers from their position on the round table where they sat. "Some toys are dangerous."

"That's right, Anthony," encouraged Gretchen.

Brittany flounced a little as she shifted in her chair. "Some are very expensive, like my collection of Jewels Junkets."

Gretchen smiled, trying to ignore the itch on her arm. She had noticed before that some very smart kids didn't know how they sounded to others. "That is correct, Brittany. However, it might be better to just mention a few expensive toys, instead of saying that you owned some."

Brittany looked like she might want to argue about that, but Gretchen continued without pausing, "Some might think you were bragging." She noticed this didn't seem to make an impression on Brittany. "Also, you never know who might be listening. A thief might overhear you." That made enough of an impression, that Brittany fell thoughtfully silent.

There was something like a snort from Janella. "Yea, and toys are sometimes used to bribe or lure kids into bad situations – kidnapping and stuff."

Gretchen looked closely at Janella. The nurse had purchased a few pairs of clothes at the Salvation Army Store in Burlington and started letting Janella change into them at school. This hadn't completely solved the odor problem, so she had also purchased soap and shampoo and let the girl shower in the restroom next to the gym. What exactly did Janella mean by "and stuff?" Was that related to her situation? Had she ever been lured or bribed?

The next day Gretchen arranged to go in to work a little early so she had time to talk to the school counselor before her classes started. That conversation didn't ease her mind about Janella's situation. The counselor said, "Janella's mom is in prison on a drug charge. Her father is dead. We've discovered that she is living with her stepdad who somehow escaped a conviction of his own in the same situation that sent her mom to prison. Please, keep me informed of anything that would indicate that stepdad is abusive – or not."

Gretchen went back to her storeroom and started loading her

art cart. They had finished the unit on design and were starting one on drawing people. Paper, pencils, and mirrors joined an assortment of portraits cut from magazines. Some grades would be sketching from life-models -- one of their classmates. Some would be drawing their own faces, using the mirrors. Others would cut one of the magazine faces in half and try to draw the other half. The youngest kids would follow step-by-step directions by Gretchen, as she also explained how to create different expressions when drawing people.

She smiled. She was sure that the classroom teachers would like the drawing lessons. Sometimes art class was noisy and messy, and, with Gretchen going to the different classrooms this year, that could be hard for the classroom teachers to handle. Drawing classes were quiet, because the kids really had to concentrate. They were also neat, because Gretchen seldom let them use erasers.

On the way home, Gretchen stopped for some groceries. She also selected a couple of products which she hoped would help with those itchy spots which she seemed to be getting more of every day. She thought about the day as she continued home. Yes, there had been the expected complaints about not using erasers. Again, she had patiently explained that erasing often got in the way of the drawing process and that, believe it or not, one "wrong" line would not ruin a picture. Several of her students showed artistic promise, including Janella. Several had problems moving beyond their stereotyped drawings. Some girls drew heavily made-up model types. Some boys drew bulging muscle action figures. Some kids drew every person with the same silly smile, but that wasn't the case with Janella. Janella's self portrait had looked depressed. Gretchen sighed as she turned onto her street and parked the car.

Ben greeted Gretchen at the door and ushered her into the living room where Gretchen's mom sat visiting with neighbor Mrs. Carmine. "Hello, everyone!" declared Gretchen. Then she noticed that the two older women had laps filled with fabric pieces.

"Good afternoon, Mrs. Parks," answered Dorine. "Ethel and I have decided to work on some hospice quilts together."

"Oh?" Gretchen was trying to digest this news.

"Yes," Ben added. "Mrs. Carmine and Mom Gunther went with me to church today, because they were thinking about joining the Comfort Quilters group."

Ethel Gunther looked slightly confused, but happy, when Gretchen glanced her way.

"I don't know how often we'll feel like going to the meetings," continued Mrs. Carmine, "especially when winter weather sets in. However, the two of us can work together." She glanced at Ethel. "I think it will be fun!"

Ethel nodded. "I can cut squares and hand-stitch them together."

Gretchen's eyebrows rose. This was the first time he mother had indicated an interest in any projects of her own. "What are the quilts used for?" she asked.

"We give them to the hospice program or the cancer care program at one of the local hospitals," answered Mrs. Carmine.

"Isn't that a great project?" Ben encouraged.

Gretchen nodded. "It is. Thank you, Mom and Mrs. C for your willingness to help."

The ladies bent back over their work, while Ben motioned Gretchen into the kitchen. "I hope you don't mind my encouraging your mom and our neighbor to do this. It just seemed that both women needed a purpose to keep them going at their best," Ben murmured close to Gretchen's ear.

Gretchen smiled. "I think it's a great idea. Mom hasn't shown any signs that it would be dangerous for her, and Mrs. Carmine's life has been pretty empty, I think, since her husband died."

"Yes. He died of cancer, so quilting for Hospice struck a chord with her."

The ladies popped a couple more pain relieving tablets the next day to help with aching fingers, but they kept working. Within a week, they had one quilt top all pieced. It was a simple checkerboard pattern, but the blue, green, and gold fabrics looked beautiful. Ben took it to the quilting ladies at church to assemble with the batting and backing. Gretchen then took the two to a fabric store to see if they could find some material for their next project. They came home with an assortment of pretty cottons – most from the clearance tables. Enough to make three more quilt tops.

During that time Gretchen started to search in earnest for the source of her skin irritation. She did some extra vacuuming, and dusting. She wiped down counters and walls and ran an air purifier. Her efforts did seem to help a little.

Gretchen started relaxing as she came home from work again. Teaching still had some challenges this year. She'd adapted to the art cart process, and she and Mr. Grabel had figured out a way of working out of the same space. However, Janella's second people-drawing project sent Gretchen trucking down to the school's counselor.

The counselor looked quietly at Janella's work. "This is a remarkable picture," she commented.

"Yes, Janella has lots of talent," agreed Gretchen. Then she went on to explain, "First, the class did self-portraits using mirrors. Next, they were supposed to do an interpretive composition of themselves in a setting that somehow defined them or was important to them."

"Hmm," the counselor responded noncommittally. "Did the student tell you what she wanted the picture to mean?"

Gretchen sighed. "Yes and no. She never referred to the female character as herself, but she did give me an explanation. She said that Wonder Woman was being attacked by her arch enemy and the bad guy was winning."

The counselor nodded. "And Wonder Woman has frizzy light hair and blazing green eyes."

"Like Janella."

"Like Janella." The counselor shifted her focus to the dark figure towering over Wonder Woman. "I wonder who her arch enemy is."

Both women stared silently at the sinister cartoon figure. The counselor glanced at Gretchen. "Have you ever met Janella's stepfather?"

Gretchen shook her head.

"I have – once – last year. This could be… I'm not sure…"

Gretchen held her breath.

"I wonder when her mother gets out of prison."

Gretchen shook her head.

"Well, I want to thank you for bringing this to me. I think I'll take a photo of this, so you can give it back to Janella. I'll call her in to my office to talk about… talk about reading to some kindergartners… and whatever else comes up."

CHAPTER 7

The counselor started meeting with Janella a couple of times each week, taking her down as a helper for the kindergartners and keeping her a few extra minutes just to chat. She made sure that she did not pull Janella out of art class or her problem solving group, since those were Janella's two favorite activities in school. Once another teacher complained to Gretchen about how much time Janella was missing from her class. Gretchen sighed, took a second deep breath, and said, "Janella is smart enough she will be able to teach herself most of what she is missing – when her head and heart are in the right place. If those aren't taken care of right now, we may lose her completely." The other teacher turned away, thoughtfully quiet.

Gretchen's mom and neighbor finished three more quilt tops, and a woman from church brought over some fabric from her own mother's house. "Mom can't sew anymore," the woman told Gretchen, "and she's happy to have this put to good use."

Gretchen also called her teacher-friend Betsy, whose husband had become ill. "They've made a diagnosis…" she hesitated. "It seems to be more mental than physical, though the mind is part of the body."

"Certainly," responded Gretchen.

"Anyway, he's on medication. He's been given some strict instructions about how to treat me, like not calling constantly when I am at work."

"Oh?"

"Yes, you see… one of his symptoms seemed to be a fearful paranoia. He somehow thought I was sneaking around and keeping secrets from him."

"I've heard of that happening before," responded Gretchen,

sensing the embarrassment in her friend's voice.

"Yes, paranoia can be one of the personality changes associated with some kinds of – of dementia."

Gretchen heard her friend's sigh over the phone. "Is that what you have been dealing with?"

"Oh, Gretchen, yes! It has been awful. My husband would say such things – things that weren't true, but he believed them! I was so afraid that it would affect my job – or someone else's reputation." There was a hint of a sob in her voice. "He's still in denial about some things, but at least has been willing to do what the doctor says."

"Are you going to be able to come back to work?" asked Gretchen. "I am enjoying the problem solving groups, but know that you would do the job better."

"Speaking of problem solving, how is Janella doing?"

"I wondered if you would ask that," replied Gretchen with a chuckle. Then, she spoke seriously. "Janella is doing well in the problem solving group and in art – but her work sometimes reminds me of Vincent van Gogh -- no, more like Frida Kahlo. Very dark and disturbing. The school counselor is working with her."

"Good!" said Betsy Moth. "I am going to try to come back next week, just for the problem solving groups. If that works out, then I'll try a little more the following week. I've got a carpenter who is going to work on some projects around our house while I'm gone. That way Jack will be distracted and have someone with him."

"Good idea. Let me know if we can be of help in some way. If your husband would be willing, Ben could take him on some service projects – delivering lunches – that kind of thing."

When Betsy did make it to school for the problem solving groups, she reviewed the work the groups had done on their first topic of *toys*. "I am really impressed with this brainstorming list of purposes of toys," she declared with a thumbs-up sign. "You've got a good list of reasons that the manufacturers would give for their products, plus some reasons

I would put in very different categories like 'ways to use up your allowance' and 'things for the dog to bury in your yard.'"

Brittany giggled. "That last one was Mrs. Parks' idea."

"Well, you know that on the practice problems the coaches can help, but don't become dependent upon us. When it comes to the competition you are on your own, so practice using your perspectives scope and look at each situation from different points of view." She flipped through several pages of work and stopped at the last section, taking time to read it carefully. "You have a good start on your plan of action," She paused. "You address several different kinds of toys that could be recycled or repurposed, but how are you going to get people to do this? Will recyclers take broken toys? The action plan isn't done until it is detailed enough for anyone to read and follow."

"But we don't know all this stuff!" said Anthony.

Mrs. Moth smiled at him and replied, "That's what research is about – finding out what you need to know, but don't know yet."

After the session, Betsy and Gretchen talked for a bit.

"You've done well with the groups," said Betsy. "I hope you won't think that you're out of a job because I can come back at least sometimes."

"It would be fine with me to let go of the problem solving groups, except..."

"Except that you get attached to the kids you work with in small groups."

Gretchen nodded. "I'd probably be bugging you about Janella all year."

"Well, my situation is still iffy enough that I want you to stay to help. Mr. Mitchell has agreed to that, and you've got your schedule set up."

Gretchen chuckled. "That's true. I also wouldn't mind actually working with another teacher for a change. Many of the teachers have meetings or team-teach part of the time. But I've been a solo act, as an art teacher."

"Teaching the problem solving groups has been a solo act for me, also." Betsy paused, cleared her throat, and went on, "Right now I feel very alone in other areas of my life and I would really appreciate someone to share this with."

Gretchen gave her friend a hug before they left for the day.

Betsy averaged making it to school about four days per week. There was the occasional emergency, and several planned appointments, but most of the time even Gretchen would have had a hard time telling that anything was wrong, because Mrs. Moth would, as she said, "Put my worries in my take-home folder and forget about them during the day."

They started another study topic in problem solving. This one was about *pollution*. In their first brainstorming session, Janella added methamphetamine fumes from drug production. This time it was Betsy Moth who talked to the school counselor about her concerns.

Ethel and Dorine continued to make quilt tops. The number of finished quilts the church ladies group turned over to the cancer care center doubled because of their efforts.

Ben's work at church also seemed to fall into a comfortable routine of board meetings, training sessions, and sermon preparation. One evening he commented that there had been fewer emergencies related to the church than he could remember in his time as a pastor.

There had also been several more meetings of the Quad Cities United Mission Group, and two different projects were beginning to form. One was a construction and tutoring trip to the Philippines which was being organized by one of the pastors with a connection to a school there. That would probably not take place until at least the next spring. The other was fix-up work and service to the community around Sylvia's church in Kansas City. After Ben brought the church's mission statement, the group had an internet conference with Brother Manuel and decided that they could help in ways that were directly evangelizing *and* support a good Christian ministry. Ben was pleased to note that both the more liberal and more conservative members in the group could agree on this one. It was also close enough and inexpensive enough that the planning and preparation were simpler. Several weekend trips were set up to accommodate working parishioners, the first one being the weekend after Thanksgiving.

When Ben told Gretchen about the time of the first trip, she mused, "We will see who is willing to give up shopping and football to do this."

One weekend in October, their daughter Anna came down with her husband Mark and their baby daughter Flora. Ethel loved watching her great-granddaughter Flora play with blocks and dolls in the middle of the Park's living room floor. Mark seemed preoccupied with messages from his office on Saturday, but Anna convinced him to leave his cell phone at the house when they went to church Sunday morning. After service, they all drove to Burlington for a dinner in the restaurant by the river. By the end of the meal, Ben and Gretchen were glad to see that Mark seemed to reconnect with his wife and daughter. When they got back to the parsonage, Mark even packed his phone in a suitcase for the trip home.

November arrived and with it the season's first snowfall. On the first Sunday of the month, a light skiff of snow covered the ground, but melted on paved roadways. Ben responded by making sure both of their vehicles had heavy quilts and window scrapers in the back seat and a small shovel and sand in the trunk. During the night two days later, strong winds brought with them five inches of snow blown into incredible drifts. Ethel and Dorine missed one day of piecing quilts together, but Ben shoveled a path between their two houses even before he shoveled the front walkway. So the very next day Ethel made her way, supported by Ben, to her neighbor's home.

School was canceled on Wednesday, when Gretchen didn't work, but not Thursday. Gretchen allowed more than twice as much time to drive there. It was one time she was very glad she went in later in the morning – and that she had that heavy quilt laid across the back seat. She noticed that Janella did not make it to school at all the rest of the week. When Janella returned the following Monday, she looked like she was ill and sat just staring in front of her during art class. The school counselor looked Gretchen up between the last two classes of the day.

"Every teacher Janella has had today has complained about her. In fact, you are the only one who didn't send her to the office or give her a detention."

"I could tell something was wrong. This is the first time she hasn't produced any art during one of my classes – it seems to be her natural way of expressing herself."

"What do you think the problem is?"

"I think something happened during, or just before, her absence from school. Probably at home. I don't want to think about what that might have been."

The counselor pursed her lips and walked away as the bell for the last class rang.

CHAPTER 8

Ben busied himself with preparations for the mission trip to Kansas City. He was in charge of gathering tools, so he created a checklist of things that were needed, had the others mark which items they could bring, and then asked if his church men could loan or donate tools – clearly marked with their names if they wanted them back. The quilting ladies stopped their regular work long enough to sew up a bunch of carpenter's belts for each mission team member. One lady even purchased some big plastic tubs to hold the tools. The group planned on driving to Kansas City after Thanksgiving dinner at noon with their families. That way they would have two full days to work.

Gretchen bought her Thanksgiving turkey – a small one – because Anna and Mark were going to his folks for the holiday, so it would just be the four of them. They had invited Mrs. Carmine.

School was only going to be held on Monday and Tuesday of that week; since she didn't work on Mondays, Gretchen had plenty of time to help Ben make last-minute preparations for his trip. She planned a simple lesson for all of her art students which involved creating "Thank You" cards from left-over supplies from other projects. Their assignment was then to give the cards to someone over the Thanksgiving holiday.

Tuesday morning came. Ethel was excited because she and Dorine were working on a secret special project. She had written a note to herself which she kept in her pocket to remind herself, but she wouldn't show the note to Gretchen. Gretchen figured it was probably a Christmas gift, so she didn't pry.

Usually Ethel didn't go over to Mrs. Carmine's until just before Gretchen left for school at about ten fifteen. Today, though, she was ready to head over before nine. Gretchen walked to Mrs. Carmine's roses at the edge of her property, then stood and watched Ethel make her way to her friend's back door. She saw Ethel knock, then wait. Ethel knocked again. She glanced back at Gretchen and shrugged. Gretchen shrugged back. Ethel reached out and pushed on the door. Maybe Dorine had called to her from inside, thought Gretchen. Ethel looked over her shoulder at Gretchen and gave a little wave. Gretchen waved back and turned to go back to her house.

A screen door banged.

"Gretchen! Come now!" Ethel's voice ended in a sort of screech.

"Coming." Gretchen spun around quickly and dashed toward her neighbor's back porch. She met her mother on the porch and slowed down enough to assess that Ethel was all right. Ethel pointed inside, so Gretchen opened the door for her mom, entering immediately after her.

Dorine Carmine sat slumped in a chair at the kitchen table. Fabric, scissors, and pins were scattered over the table and the floor. Mrs. Carmine tried to turn at the sound of their entry, but started to fall from her chair. Gretchen pushed her upright in the chair and held her around the shoulders.

"Mrs. Carmine, are you alright?"

Dorine wobbled her head and tried to say something. Gretchen couldn't understand her words, but assumed that they meant that she wasn't all right. "Can you smile?" Mrs. Carmine's smile was definitely lopsided. Gretchen figured that she didn't need to go through the other stroke signs. She turned to her mother. "Do you know where her bathroom is, Mom?"

Ethel nodded.

"Can you get me a bottle of aspirin?"

Ethel scurried off, repeating "*aspirin, aspirin, aspirin*" to herself.

Gretchen stayed behind Mrs. Carmine, but whipped her phone out, then hesitated. She dialed Ben's cell number. When Ben answered, Gretchen said, "Ben, I think Mrs. C. has had a stroke. Mom has gone to get aspirin. I'm making sure she doesn't fall. I started to call 911, but thought it's going to take a while for an ambulance to get here. So, I called you."

"I'm in my car. I can be there in ten minutes," said Ben. "Go ahead and call 911, but we'll start out if they don't arrive before we can take off."

Ethel came back with a bottle of baby aspirin. Gretchen placed one at a time in Mrs. Carmine's mouth. After several had dissolved in her mouth, Gretchen said a silent prayer and put a spoon filled with water in Dorine's mouth. The swallowing reflex seemed to work, so Gretchen gave her another spoonful. Then Gretchen turned her attention as to how they could move her.

"Mom, bring me that scarf," Said Gretchen, nodding.

Ethel brought a long winter scarf hung over a jacket by the back door. Gretchen slipped it around Dorine just under her arms, wrapped it around the back of the chair, weaving it through the spokes on the back, and tied it. Ethel had by that time come up with another scarf and tied it around Dorine's legs and under the seat of the chair.

"Coat," said Gretchen.

Ethel trotted to the front closet and got a long, quilted winter coat which Gretchen wrapped over Mrs. Carmine like a blanket. Just then they heard feet on the back porch and Ben came through the door. He went right up to Mrs. Carmine and knelt to look her in the eyes.

"Mrs. C, do you understand that we need to get you to the hospital?"

Dorine Carmine nodded and mumbled, "Yea."

"I'm going to bring my car around to the front of your house. If the ambulance isn't here by then, we'll tip this chair and scoot you to the car..." He turned toward Gretchen and whispered, "Good work on tying her in. I'm not sure how we'll get her from the chair to the car, but we'll do our best."

Ben turned back to Dorine. "Before I go, I'm going to take just a minute to pray – I think we all need it."

Dorine nodded. Ethel and Gretchen gathered in close.

"Dear God," started Ben. "Thank you for arranging things so well this far. Mrs. C. wasn't here by herself for a long time. You have helped my family to be where they needed to be to help. Now, please, help us get her to the hospital safely – and, God, you can start healing her even before we get there if you don't mind."

As they lifted their heads they heard a siren in the distance. Ben smiled. "Well, it looks like the experts are going to get here!"

A few minutes later the EMTs had Mrs. C. arranged in the ambulance, started the siren and headed off.

"W-Wait!" stuttered Ethel. "Call them back! I want to go with my friend!"

"I'll take you," Ben said, putting an arm around his mother-in-law's shoulder. He turned to Gretchen. "Are you coming?"

Gretchen glanced at her watch. "10:25! I – I haven't called anyone at school and I'm going to be late if I don't leave right now!"

"Then go," responded Ethel. "Ben and I can handle this. You can swing by the hospital on your way home."

Gretchen nodded and was off, dashing to get her things and to her car. She speed dialed the school and let Mary know very briefly that she had been delayed but would be there ASAP.

It was hard to keep her mind on her work that day, but Gretchen knew that her mom and Ben and the hospital's staff could do more than she could have done. So, she tried to put the problem in her "take-home folder" to worry about later.

The teacher of her first class was glad to see her walk in a few minutes late. "I'm glad you are here! The kids will probably get more out of art today than they will most of their other classes."

Gretchen smiled and turned to the class, apologizing for being late. The kids in that first class seemed to enjoy the project and created several excellent cards. The same went for the next two classes. The class that she met with right after lunch seemed especially squirrelly; they couldn't settle down and the cards were done rather haphazardly. Then Gretchen had the eighth graders. Janella's reaction really surprised Gretchen. She refused to fold her card paper and chose only three colors of scraps: black, gray, and red. She tore the pieces into rough shapes and pasted them, layer upon layer, covering the whole card and extending beyond its edges. On the back she turned it over and wrote in all capitals: THANKS FOR NOTHING.

Gretchen did not want to make a scene in front of the other kids, so she waited until the end of class and called Janella out in the hall. "Janella, I couldn't help noticing that you seemed upset." *That's an understatement*, she thought. "Can you tell me what the problem is?"

Janella shook her head.

"Can I help in any way?"

Janella glanced up at Gretchen. Tears brimmed in the corners of her eyes. "I don't think so, Mrs. Parks. I..." She stopped, looked at the floor and shook her head.

"Would it help to talk to our school counselor?" Gretchen asked.

Janella shook her head violently, then said, "She's sick today. She's not here."

"Oh..."

"Look, don't bother about me, I'm just – me." Janella turned to go back into her class.

Gretchen spoke just loud enough for her to hear. "And that *me* is pretty special."

Another class was waiting, so Gretchen hurried on, remembering that there would be a problem challenge meeting after school where she could check on Janella again.

Janella wasn't at that meeting and, with the jubilant affirmation of the rest of the team, all kids who walked to school, Mrs. Moth dismissed the meeting after passing out a vocabulary crossword to "keep them learning" over the break. As the students dashed out an announcement came over the loudspeaker system: "Teachers may leave as soon as the students they are responsible for have gone. Have a great Thanksgiving." Both teachers breathed a sigh of relief and hurried to gather their belongings.

Gretchen put a silk scarf around her neck to protect another red welt from the fuzz on her coat. She was only taking home her project planning book, so that she could finish her lesson plans for the coming week. She tossed it into the back seat, noting that her emergency blanket had fallen to the floor.

Her mind was already on the trip to the hospital, so she didn't worry about refolding the quilt across the back seat.

She did think about checking her phone for messages and found one from Ben which had been sent about an hour ago. It said: "Mrs. C transferred to Iowa City by ambulance. We are going home to get clothes etc. Then to I.C."

Gretchen called Ben's number. When he answered, and assured her he wasn't driving, she asked, "What should I do?"

"Mom Gunther and I are just getting ready to leave our house. We've gotten clothes for everyone, including you and Mrs. Carmine. We've picked up reading material and locked up both houses."

"That sounds Like I don't need to come home."

"Exactly. From where we are, going up to I-80 and over will be the fastest. If you are still at school, highway 34 and up would be a quicker route."

"O.K. I'll just head for Iowa City then."

With the road improvements done over the last several years, the trip through Burlington and northwest toward Iowa City's University Hospital was relatively quick and easy. In just a little over an hour and a half later she pulled into one of the hospital parking lots.

Following signs, she made her way to the emergency department. Arriving at the information window, she asked about Dorine Carmine. The man at the counter said that he would go check to see if she could go back to see her, and walked the other way. Gretchen wandered around the waiting room for several minutes before the man reappeared and escorted her back to Mrs. Carmine's examination room.

Dorine Carmine lay on a narrow bed with her head and legs slightly elevated. She turned her head and tried to smile as Gretchen came in the room. The smile was less lopsided than before. "Goo to shee oo," She said.

"It's good to see you," responded Gretchen.

"Jus leff me ear," continued Dorine.

"I'm sure they will be back, but I'm here now. So you won't be alone."

Dorine nodded and closed her eyes. Gretchen pulled a chair

up close to her bed, so that Mrs. Carmine could see her if she opened them. It did seem a long time before anyone returned to the room. At one point Dorine opened her eyes and coughed. Indicating that her mouth was dry, Gretchen picked up a cup with a straw in it and let her sip a little water. Then Dorine closed her eyes again and went back to sleep.

The registration man opened the door once more, and Gretchen was thrilled to see her mother and Ben quietly enter. The man brought in two more chairs so that everyone had a place to sit, and he did it so quietly that Dorine continued to sleep.

Ben wrote on a notepad: "How is she doing?"

Gretchen wrote back: "Maybe a little better. Haven't seen the doctor yet."

Ethel shook her head and frowned. She motioned for the pad. "Hurry up and wait."

Both Ben and Gretchen smiled and nodded. Ben got out a book to read. Gretchen pulled out a coloring book of exotic flowers and offered it to her mom, after tearing out a page for herself. Out came colored pencils and the two women worked quietly.

Finally a doctor and nurse came in, and, at the sound of their arrival, Mrs. Carmine opened her eyes.

"Hello, hello, hello!" said the male doctor with over-exuberance. He referred to the screen of the computer tablet he held in one hand. "Well, ah, my lady, it looks like you have had quite a day."

Dorine nodded and Ethel replied, "We all have."

The doctor glanced her way and nodded. "I'm sure you have. Are you family?"

Ben cleared his throat. "The closest thing she has to family. We're her next door neighbors."

Nodding the doctor rubbed his face. "No family at all?"

Dorine interrupted. "Sisser. Powof atturn."

"Can we contact her?" asked the nurse.

"Pursh," responded Dorine Carmine. "Phone."

Gretchen reached for the bag of belongings that had come with her from the Burlington hospital. She got out the purse and handed it to Dorine. Trying to lift her right hand, Dorine waved the purse away. "Ooo!"

Gretchen took a deep breath and reached for the cell phone inside a small pouch in the purse. Flicking it on, she quickly got to her neighbor's contact list and scrolled down, wondering how she would recognize the sister's name. But when she got to the S's, Gretchen saw that Dorine had solved that problem by naming one contact Sis (with her name in parentheses). She looked up. "Who should call?" she asked.

Ben reached for the phone and stepped into the hall. Soon he was talking to someone. "Mabel Morgan?"

"Yes."

"This is Ben Parks, the next door neighbor of your sister Dorine Carmine."

"The Baptist preacher?"

"Yes, the Baptist preacher. This morning your sister had a stroke and she is right now in the emergency room at the U of I hospitals."

"Oh my!"

"Yes, she is alert and able to communicate, though her speech is slurred."

"It sounds serious."

"It is, but we found her soon after it happened. My mother-in-law was going over to do some sewing with her and found her."

"Oh, good!"

"She first went to the Burlington hospital, and then she was transferred here."

"I need to get there!"

"That would be helpful, since I understand you have the medical power of attorney."

"Yes ... I do."

"Where will you be coming from?" Ben asked, trying to figure out how soon to reasonably expect her.

"Oh, distance isn't a problem! I live just south of Iowa City. It's just that – well, I have a handicapped daughter who can't be left alone and might be frightened by the hospital."

"Would you like to talk to the doctor?"

"Oh, yes!"

Ben opened the door just in time to hear the doctor say, "Now, grip my fingers as tight as you can … good."

"Doctor, I have the sister on the phone."

"Oh! Thank you." The doctor took the phone and stepped into the hall after Ben had entered.

Gretchen brought him up to date. "The doctor just went through the standard body function tests they have been repeating ever since the paramedics arrived this morning. Several of her functions have improved slightly – I can't tell about the hand squeeze thing."

"Okay."

"They are getting a room ready for her up in the Neurology ward. As soon as it's ready they will transfer her."

Ben nodded.

"Not too much will be done today, except stabilize her medically. Aspirin. Blood thinner. Watching her blood pressure very closely. Continuing to check her functions…"

Ben nodded again. "No real decisions unless there is another crisis. And they have the sister's phone number now."

The doctor came back into the room, phone in hand. "Can any of you stay until about eight or eight-thirty tonight?"

Gretchen glanced at her watch. It was already after six. She glanced at the others who were nodding. "It should be no problem."

The doctor nodded and held the phone to his ear. "Did you hear that? Good. Goodbye." He handed the phone back to Ben as he continued, "She will come just as soon as she has put her daughter to bed. Her husband will be home before then, but she is most concerned with disturbing her daughter's bedtime routine."

As the doctor turned to leave, a gurney rolled up outside the door to the room. Ben, Gretchen, and Ethel moved into the hall to be out of the way as the hospital personnel worked to transfer Mrs. Carmine to the rolling cot so that they could take her to her room.

"Why don't you and Mom Gunther go get something to eat," suggested Ben. "I can text you with the room number so that you can come up when you are finished."

"That sounds like a good idea!" replied the nurse. "I've got a map of the hospital I can give you which has the room and directions marked on it."

"Wow, thanks," replied Gretchen.

Ben followed Mrs. Carmine's gurney while Ethel and Gretchen turned off at the sign for the cafeteria.

The cafeteria was noisy and busy. Gretchen glanced over at her mother and noticed a stressed look on her face. Ethel had been holding up remarkably well as she tried to "be there" for her friend, but it was obvious she was worn out.

Remembering the breakfast on the train, Gretchen looked around for something that both she and her mom liked. There were egg salad sandwiches. Ethel agreed that those looked good, so they both put one on their tray. There were cooked green beans. Again, both asked for a serving. As they passed the deserts, one giant piece of coconut cream pie made Ethel pause.

"My, that looks tasty," declared Ethel, "But it is far too big a piece for me to eat!"

"Would you like to split a piece, Mom? We could share it?"

"That sounds perfect," declared Gretchen's mom.

Two cold glasses of milk finished their meals. They checked out and headed for a table.

Ethel was rather quiet during the meal, but Gretchen realized that she felt like concentrating on her food, also. It was when they got to the sharing of the pie that Ethel perked up. Gretchen carefully cut the pie in half and put the slightly smaller piece on her own plate, carefully passing the other half to her mother.

Ethel perked up and smiled. Putting the first bite in her mouth, Ethel closed her eyes and savored the taste. "I do like a good coconut cream pie!" she declared.

"I do too, Mom. Thanks for suggesting it."

They slowly finished their pie and took the trays to the appropriate conveyor belt. Then taking out the map the nurse had given them, Gretchen and Ethel headed toward elevator E and took it to the sixth floor. Ethel stayed close to her daughter, but seemed to be somewhat recovered after eating the pie.

They found the door to Mrs. Carmine's room closed and Ben standing outside.

"They're cleaning her up. Help for the bathroom didn't come in time – if they could have helped her even then, she's so limited. Anyway, they seemed to be used to this with stroke patients."

Ethel looked concerned.

Ben noticed her expression and added, "I have already seen improvement in her symptoms since this morning, however, so I am hopeful that this very limited time will be short-lived."

The door opened and three people in medical uniforms, rolling a large container, came out. One motioned and said, "She's ready for company."

Dorine Carmine's first words were, "Frustatin' to nee so mush help!"

Ethel made sympathetic noises.

"Was you supper goo?" asked Dorine.

Ethel looked blank for a moment, then brightened. "We had coconut cream pie for desert!"

"Mmm!"

Ben saw Gretchen motion from the chair where she had parked herself. When he got closer, she murmured, "That pie made quite an impression – and she's even remembered that she ate it fifteen minutes later."

Ben positioned another chair in the room in a comfortable spot for Ethel to sit and visit with her friend. Then he left for his turn at the cafeteria.

Gretchen leaned back, resting her head on the back cushions of the chair and closed her eyes. Ethel and Dorine chatted about doctors and hospitals for a few minutes, but pretty soon they were dozing also. About forty-five minutes after leaving, Ben returned with a supper cart following right behind.

The head of Dorine's bed was raised, another pillow placed behind her, and the food tray pushed into position across the bed. As the food worker left, the nurse entered. She was just in time to watch Dorine bow her head in prayer. After the prayer the nurse smiled and said, "I'm just here to see how you do with the first few bites of food. You did well with your swallow test earlier, but I thought I'd be here at the start of your meal."

Mrs. Carmine reached slowly and carefully with her left hand and took a drink through a straw. It went down fine. Then she sampled the mashed potatoes. That she could also swallow well. Finally she took a bite of her hamburger and chewed. No problems. The nurse smiled, nodded, and left the room.

Dorine Carmine turned to Ethel and said, "I wi never take eatin so mush for granty agin."

Ethel nodded her understanding.

"Thish tases so good!"

Dorine was through with her meal and being helped to use a commode when a younger version of that lady hurried up the hall. Ben reached out his hand to her, saying, "You have got to be related to Dorine Carmine."

The middle-aged woman rolled her eyes and replied, "Is it that obvious."

Gretchen chuckled. "Yes, but I would have guessed you for a daughter, not a sister."

The woman perked up at that. "I was Mamma's change of life 'accident.' She was always careful to tell me it was the best accident that ever happened to her, though." She turned to Ethel. "You must be Dorine's quilting friend."

Ethel beamed at being known.

"Just to be sure we're all on the same page, I am Mabel Morgan – Dorine's baby sister and medical power of attorney.

"My youngest is safely asleep with my husband at home to watch. He doesn't work tomorrow, so I don't have to worry about when I get home. I will stay as long as I am needed tomorrow." She frowned thoughtfully. "From what the doctor said, Sis is probably going to be here several days at least..."

"Yes," said Ben. "I don't think you need to worry about anything past the hospital stay for several days. I've seen improvement even today, but she's being helped by three people to use the bathroom right now. They are working to stabilize her blood pressure and discussing tests for tomorrow."

Gretchen thought the mother might be thinking about the nearness of the Thanksgiving holiday and how this would affect it. "Do you have plans for Thanksgiving?"

"Yes – no. I mean, we're not going anywhere. One of the older kids was bringing their family down, but ..."

"They won't be doing much on Thanksgiving here at the hospital," Ben said.

"We could visit her," added Ethel.

Ben turned to Gretchen with an unspoken question. Gretchen responded. "Yes, this is a different kind of Thanksgiving for us. Ben is leaving on a short mission trip to Kansas City in the early afternoon. We could easily drive over here for a visit."

"Oh, that would be a big help!" declared Mabel.

As Ben, Gretchen, and Ethel walked down the hall toward parking ramp 4, they discussed their plans for the next day. Gretchen had fixed all except a few of the simplest items for their meal tomorrow. With just the three of them, she had frozen much of the turkey for later use. After an early lunch, they would drive Ben to his mission rendezvous point in the Quad Cities and then head toward Iowa City.

Reaching the entrance to the parking ramp, Gretchen gave a start.

"What is it?" asked Ben.

Gretchen was searching the shadows of the parking area with her eyes. "I guess it was nothing. I saw – or thought I saw – a child – a girl – right over there. I don't see her now."

"Is it one of that family down there?" asked Ethel.

Gretchen shook her head. "I guess it must have been, but none of them look like who I thought I saw."

Ben cocked his head to one side. "Who did you think you saw?"

Gretchen gave something between a laugh and a sigh. "I thought I saw one of my best students." She paused, and then decided to explain a little more. "Also, one with the most problems."

The three peered once again around the parking area.

Gretchen shrugged. "Well, maybe it was a trick of the lighting. She's not here now."

They continued on to their cars. It was decided that probably

the best route back would be the southern route through
Burlington. Ethel would ride with her daughter and Ben would
drive back alone. Ben helped his mother-in-law into the front
passenger's seat, gave Gretchen a parting kiss, and hurried on
to his car in the next aisle.

With Ben following Gretchen's car, the family started on
their way home. A few flakes swirled around them as they
turned from highway 218 to 34 East. It was quiet in the car,
except for the sound of Ethel snoring and shifting in her seat.
She had dozed off almost immediately, but the snoring came
intermittently. Gretchen chuckled at some of the strange sounds
her mother made as she slept. Occasionally a snort sounded
more like a groan or a cough, and once there was a sound that
reminded Gretchen of someone turning over in bed. She
couldn't figure out how her mother had made that sound.

The flakes had stopped by the time they crossed the
Mississippi into Illinois. Ethel started to wake up about the
time they turned north again. By the time Gretchen pulled into
their detached garage, both mother and daughter were eager to
get inside and get to bed.

Ben pulled up right behind them and came around to help his
mother-in-law out of the car and into the house safely. A small
skiff of snow on the pavement made the sidewalk connecting
the house and garage a little slick. Gretchen started to lock the
car doors, but Ben said, "I'll come back for the suitcase in a
minute."

Gretchen nodded and headed to unlock the back door.
Inside, Ethel turned toward the downstairs bathroom and
Gretchen climbed the stairs to the upstairs one. Ben did a quick
inventory of the house to make sure everything was all right
before heading back out to the garage.

Suitcase inside and the backdoor locked, all three breathed
a sigh of relief and started preparations for bed.

Knowing that Ethel sometimes lost her orientation if her
day was too unusual, Ben left the door of their bedroom
upstairs open so that they could better hear unusual sounds
from below.

In the middle of the night Gretchen and Ben were both

awakened by the sound of Ethel's voice. What she was saying made little sense however.

"Who's that sleeping in my bed!" declared Ethel in a voice which made Gretchen flashback to bedtime fairy tales during her childhood. "Why, it's Goldilocks herself."

At this point Gretchen was half way down the stairs and could see into their living room. "Mom, that's not your bed, that's the sofa," Gretchen called.

Ethel turned and replied, "But I am right about Goldilocks."

Gretchen was almost at her side now and stopped in her tracks as she saw what had surprised her confused mother. There on the sofa, rubbing her eyes and looking both tired and scared was Janella.

CHAPTER 9

"Janella!" Gretchen exclaimed.

Ben murmured to his wife, "Your problem-solving student?"

Gretchen nodded. She took a moment to control herself, so she wouldn't frighten the girl further. "What are you doing here, honey?"

That impish grin flitted across Janella's face. "Well, until a minute ago I was sleeping – until great-grandma bear woke me up."

Ben stifled a snort.

So did Gretchen. "I mean, I don't remember being asked if you could come for a visit."

Janella's face became serious. "I didn't ask. I didn't want to go home with my stepdad for five days."

Gretchen tilted her head forward in a half nod.

"When he's doing drugs and partying with his friends I try to avoid all of them. That would be very hard to do for five days."

Ben stepped forward a little. "Why do you try to avoid him, Janella?"

Janella sighed. "I'm scared of him. Usually he just ignores me, but sometimes…"

"Has he ever hurt you?" asked Gretchen.

Janella frowned. "I'm not sure what to say. He's never beat me, but some of the stuff… I don't like it."

Ethel spoke up. "I always thought there was more to Goldilocks' behavior than just the desire to explore the bears' house."

It was Janella who burst out laughing. "That story didn't sound quite right to me, either," she finally said. She flipped her legs down, so she was sitting upright on the couch and began to look more relaxed.

Ben sat down across from her, and Gretchen sat down in another chair. Surprisingly, Janella patted the couch next to her. "You can sit here, Great-grandma Bear." Ethel did that.

When all were settled, Ben put his hands together and leaned on his knees in a relaxed position. "Janella, we need to understand more about why and how you got here."

"Well – technically – Mrs. Parks brought me."

Gretchen's eyes narrowed. "That blanket on the floor of my car?"

"Yes, I was underneath it."

"That couldn't have been very comfortable," commented Ben.

Curls bobbled as Janella shook her head. "No, sir, it wasn't. But I wanted to get away without being found out."

"I guess it worked," commented Gretchen.

Janella chuckled nervously. "Yes, but I didn't expect you to drive so far! I thought you probably lived in Burlington and I could just slip out and stay in the woods around town."

"Our neighbor had a stroke this – no, yesterday morning. She ended up being taken to Iowa City."

Janella nodded her head. "I know. I needed to go to the bathroom, so I found my way into the hospital. Since it was kinda cold outside, I decided to stay inside, but where I could keep an eye out for you returning."

"So I really did see you ahead of us in the parking garage?"

Janella nodded. "Yes, the family in front of me was very slow! I thought you'd catch up with me, but I finally got around them."

Ethel yawned.

Gretchen commented, "You can go back to bed if you like, Mom. We shouldn't be too much longer."

"And miss all this excitement!" declared Ethel.

Ben smiled, but looked serious again as he turned back to Janella. "We want to help you, but we've got a predicament."

"What's a predicament?"

"A problem."

Janella nodded. "I'm a problem solver – shoot!"

"Well, we've transported you across state lines without a guardian's consent."

"What guardian? He never guarded me from nothin'.."

'That may be, but he was the adult you were living with. If he has reported your disappearance to the police, they will be searching for you."

"I don't want you to call the police! I don't want to go back home!"

Gretchen sighed. "We have to. My husband, Pastor Ben, is friends with several area police officers. He knows how to do it to minimize problems."

Janella looked suspicious. "I'm not going home! I'll run away first."

"I'll tell them that, Janella," Ben assured her. "But the first thing I will do is ask if there are any missing child reports."

"If there aren't any?"

"I don't want to say something, and it not work out that way. I'm not sure. It's late – early -- and it's a holiday. If the officers know you are safe, they probably will not rush into anything..."

Janella still looked suspicious.

Ben cleared his throat. "Why don't we all get settled again for the rest of the night? Janella, if you want to move up to our son's old room...?"

"I like it right here!"

"Then I'll get you a blanket," said Gretchen.

"Since I'm up, I'll go out and check around the house to make sure we didn't forget anything when we got home last night," Ben concluded. He checked the lock on the front door, then headed out the back door with his keys in one hand and his cell phone in the other.

Gretchen returned with both a blanket and a pillow. Janella put her head on the pillow and allowed herself to be covered up with a blanket, but she looked like she might jump up and run out the door at any moment. "If anyone knows what to do in this situation, it's Pastor Ben," remarked Gretchen almost casually.

"Yes, my son-in-law is a gem!" declared Ethel.

"So you think it's okay, Great-grandma Bear?" asked Janella.

"Why are you calling me that?" responded Ethel. "My name is Ethel Gunther."

Janella glanced toward Gretchen with a question in her eyes.

"Why don't you call my mom Grandma Ethel," replied Gretchen. "That way she will know you are referring to her. She might not always remember the Goldilocks incident."

Janella continued to look puzzled for a moment, then nodded slowly. "Oh, I get it. We studied old age dementia last year in problem solving."

Ethel drew herself up with mock severity. "If you are referring to me it is old age de-women-tia!"

Janella's mouth dropped open, while Gretchen smiled.

Gretchen addressed Janella. "Mom knows she's got some problems, but she's kept her sense of humor about life."

Ethel nodded. "That's life, take it or leave it. I'm still taking it."

Outside Ben was talking to the county sheriff. The sheriff said, "No, pastor, no reports of missing children. In fact, no one of any age has been reported missing all week."

"Thanks, sheriff," replied Ben. "I'm sorry I woke you."

"No, you did the right thing. I'll call my counterpart over in Iowa and ask them to check on Janella's stepdad. Make sure he's all right. The only problem I see with you keeping her until morning is that she might decide to run away."

"I've thought of that. I think I'm too excited to go back to sleep, so I'll sit in the kitchen and study for my next sermon."

"Don't you have a trip to leave on tomorrow."

"Yup, but I can nap."

"Well, I'll get to tracking down more info about this situation. Thanks again for calling."

Ben returned to the house, being sure to fasten the deadbolt on the back door. Then he turned to see what was happening inside. Ethel wasn't in her bed yet. She sat beside Janella, patting one hand and comforting her. "Now, you don't need to worry. You picked the right people to decide to visit. My daughter just loves kids, and her husband is a pastor. Pastors know how to help people – and if they don't they ask God to help them!"

"Thank you Grandma Ethel," said Janella.

"Well, you are welcome, I'm sure. Are you really my granddaughter?"

Janella hugged her. "Tonight I am, Grandma."

Ethel patted her hand again and got up, nodding to Ben as she passed by on her way back to her bed.

"What do you like for breakfast?" Ben asked as he walked through the living room.

Janella sat with the blanket pulled up around her neck. "Food," she said. "Food is my favorite thing to have for breakfast."

Ben nodded as he headed for the stairs. "Food there will be," he replied. "God bless you, Janella." He had decided to put her in God's hands for the rest of the night and returned to bed.

In the morning when Gretchen and Ben made it downstairs, they found Ethel and Janella just sitting down to eat. Ethel had scrambled eggs on the hotplate while Janella heated up precooked bacon in the microwave. She had already prepared toast and had butter sitting on the table, along with glasses of milk and juice.

Janella turned with a bright smile and said, "Sleepy-heads! The FOOD is ready. Grandma and I fixed it."

Ben and Gretchen found their spots at the table and, after a short prayer, all began to eat. The Parks noted that Janella consumed twice as much as the rest of them. Gretchen wondered if she had had anything to eat after her school lunch the day before. Ben breathed a sigh of relief to see that she had decided to stay for food. And warmth. And safety. Smart girl, he thought. Survival is the ultimate reason for learning problem solving.

Gretchen looked Janella over after breakfast. Her clothes were much cleaner than usual and so was she. "Janella, do you have any other clothes with you?"

"No," Janella replied. "I – I know I sometimes am pretty dirty and – and even smell. I knew that would be a problem for my escape plans, if people could smell me coming. So – so I washed one set of clothes in the bathroom sink and laid them over my heat register to dry. I got away with that without getting him suspicious, but taking a bunch of other smelly stuff wouldn't have helped." She shrugged uncomfortably.

Gretchen bit her lower lip thoughtfully. "Humm," she shook her head slightly, "you are using your problem-solving skills in real life situations."

Janella's shoulders got a little straighter.

Gretchen continued. "I think one thing we need to do this morning is get you a few more clothes. It looks like you may be away from home for several days…"

"I hope so!" cut in Janella.

Gretchen nodded. "So, you will need a few things… Toothbrush, paste, shampoo, soap – these things we have. But clothes…" She suddenly grinned. Giving Janella a quizzical look, she continued. "Of course you look about the same size as my mom…" Here Gretchen burst out laughing. "You should see your face, Janella! No, we're not going to make you wear grandma clothes. I need to do a little shopping in Burlington, and you can come along."

"Mrs. Parks, I don't want to cost you a lot of money."

"I'm glad you are sensitive to that, Janella. We'll start at the thrift shops and then fill in what we can't get there at Walmart."

Janella looked relieved. Ben stayed home with Ethel while Gretchen took Janella with her. They hit two thrift shops and found a couple of nice shirts, a pullover sweater, a decent pair of pants and a nightgown. They also picked up a warmer jacket than the one that Janella had worn to school. Janella was excited about these purchases and got even more excited when Gretchen helped her pick out a package of underwear, a sport bra, socks, and a brand new pair of jeans at Walmart. They picked up some prepared food in the foods section of the large discount store, and hurried home to provide lunch for all at home.

After lunch Janella changed into some of her new clothes, letting Gretchen wash her old ones. They played board games most of the afternoon and bundled to take a walk before supper. Janella blossomed under this peaceful family life and showed an amazing gentleness with her interactions with Ethel.

Janella insisted on sleeping on the couch again, but she wore the nightgown they had purchased that day. She also seemed to enjoy it when Ethel tucked her in and prayed with her before turning out the lights.

The next morning Janella and Ethel again fixed breakfast. They watched the Macy's Thanksgiving parade on television and Ben and Gretchen called both of their children to wish them a good day.

About eleven in the morning, Gretchen got out the food she had prepared and refrigerated for today. Some dishes were heated on the hotplate and others in the microwave. With Janella's help, the table was set and meal laid out by 11:30 a.m. Ben led the small group in a prayer of thanksgiving. Gretchen added a short one about safety for the mission trip, and they began to eat.

It was a modest meal for a Thanksgiving celebration, but Janella acted like she hadn't seen such a meal in a long time. At one point she said, "This reminds me of when we lived with Grandma Kelly in Chicago."

Ben became suddenly thoughtful. After a few moments he said, "Janella, is your grandma still alive?"

Janella looked surprised. "Well, as far as I know, she is. But I haven't seen or heard from her since Mamma got hooked up with my stepdad." Janella looked discouraged. "Now, Mom's in prison somewhere. I can't see her. I don't know how to get in touch with Grandma – if she is still alive! And I couldn't think of any safe place to be for Thanksgiving, except maybe with you guys."

Ethel reached over and patted her hand. Janella gave her a little smile and stirred the food on her plate.

Ben turned to Gretchen. "I have an idea," he murmured, patting his cell phone.

Gretchen nodded, and Ben got up from his seat. While Ben

left the room, Gretchen turned to Janella. "You picked a safe place. We will finish our meal and get Pastor Ben to his mission team before we worry about anything else."

Janella nodded, but continued to play with her food until Ethel started to tease her. "Don't you like my cooking? Or my daughter's? Are you going to insult your hosts by not eating a good meal?" If the words had come from anyone else, they might have sounded harsh, but Ethel made them sound like more like saying "I love you."

The three were just putting whipped cream on pumpkin pie when Ben strode back into the room. He had his phone in his hand, and held it out toward Janella. Janella took it and held it to her ear. "Hello?" Her face broke into a radiant smile. "Grandma!" She listened a while and looked a little disappointed, but soon the sad look was gone again, replaced by an expression of hope. Listening, but not totally understanding the conversation, it seemed to Gretchen that there was a change in Janella's accent as she spoke to her grandmother. After a few minutes Janella said goodbye, and sat down in front of her piece of pie.

"Well?" Gretchen could not contain her curiosity after Janella had stuffed three big bites of pie in her mouth without saying anything. Janella swallowed, then grinned. "Grandma is coming to see me next week – I think. She's sick today and Chicago got a lot more snow last night than we did here, but she's – she's so happy to find me! Mom did not let her know where we were, and we moved several times. Anyway, there may be someplace I can go if you guys don't want me."

Gretchen's mouth dropped open, not knowing how to respond; but Ethel did better. She immediately reached over for Janella's hand, not even letting a sticky spoon interfere with her grabbing hold of that hand. "Girl, you are wanted here! You will always be wanted! But I'm glad they found your other grandma, because you can never have too many people loving you!"

After they were finished, Ethel and Janella took care of the dishes while Ben and Gretchen packed the car. While packing, Ben filled Gretchen in on his phone search. The local police dispatcher was pleased to have something important to do on her holiday shift. She found out that, though there was no missing person's report on Janella, there was one for her mother which had just been filed using the name of her first husband. She had found it by doing a search for anyone with Janella's last name. That led her directly to Janella's paternal grandpa and grandma.

"That sounds very hopeful," responded Gretchen, "But the excuses – an illness and the weather – do you think the Grandparents had a change of heart?"

Ben smiled. "You didn't hear the grandmother's voice on the phone. She sounded sick. Also, I checked my weather app earlier today. Chicago got a foot of snow last night. Came in so quick it closed O'Hare Airport for a couple of hours."

Gretchen nodded her understanding.

"I gave her your cell number, and Grandma Kelly said that she would call when she has plans for a visit worked out."

"Okay," responded Gretchen, but with a note of uncertainty in her voice.

"Don't worry about it now," encouraged Ben. "You've got several other things to deal with for the next few days. Mrs. Carmine in the hospital. Mom Gunther. Janella." He grinned. "That should keep you busy until I return."

Ethel and Janella came out. Ethel carried a small suitcase and Janella had put some of her new clothes in a cloth grocery sack. Ben and Gretchen got in the front, with Ben driving for this first leg of their journey. Ethel and Janella shared the back seat. Along the trip to the Quad Cities meeting place, at one point Janella said, "The seats in your car are much more comfortable than the floor."

Ben and Gretchen chuckled, but Ethel said quite seriously, "Of course they are. The floor is for feet, not bottoms."

That made Janella laugh. "Bottoms! Mrs. Parks, your mom said, 'bottoms.'"

Gretchen could see in her vanity mirror that Ethel looked confused and a little hurt by Janella's laughter. "Janella, I know that you were just indulging in junior high humor, but I think you hurt Grandma Ethel's feelings. I think *she* thinks you were making fun of her."

Janella turned immediately to Ethel. "I'm sorry! I didn't mean to hurt your feelings. I just thought what you said sounded funny. I say a lot of funny things, too."

Ethel patted Janella's hand. "That's okay. You are a sweet girl."

Soon Ethel was asleep and snoring with her mouth open. Gretchen glanced over her shoulder and saw that Janella was having a hard time resisting the urge to laugh at the interesting sounds coming from her new older friend. "Have you ever been to the Quad Cities?" she asked.

Janella changed her focus from Ethel to Gretchen. "I'm not sure. If we did come here, it was just driving through."

"The most common route from Chicago to Burlington touches the edge of the communities," mentioned Ben.

"Well, maybe we did drive that way," replied Janella hesitantly. "But we stayed in a couple of other places in Illinois first before coming to Iowa."

Ben nodded, but did not pry further.

"I'm afraid you won't get to see much today, either," responded Gretchen. "After we let Ben off, we'll be heading toward Iowa City again to visit our neighbor."

"I know... and we're spending the night in a hotel so we can see her again in the morning."

"That's the plan we made before we knew you would be with us, but if that's a problem..."

"I brought my clothes and toothbrush. I'm ready for anything, Mrs. P."

Gretchen smiled. "I believe you are!" she declared.

CHAPTER 10

Ben met his team in the parking lot of a church in Moline. Gretchen, Ethel, and Janella stayed long enough to see two vans loaded up with supplies and people before they continued their journey. They soon were headed west out of the Quad Cities on interstate highway 80. It was Ethel that noticed the sign for the Herbert Hoover Presidential Museum at the Long Branch exit.

"Does that interest you, Mom?"

"People interest me," replied her mother. "And presidents are usually very interesting people."

"Have you heard of Herbert Hoover, Janella?" asked Gretchen.

"Just that he was a president before Roosevelt."

"Well, we don't have the time now, but we might see if the museum is open on our way home."

"I would like that," responded Ethel.

Gretchen made a mental note to add that to their itinerary.

They reached the hospital parking lot, and with a comment from Janella that she was glad she wouldn't have to hide in the car, they locked it and entered through the second floor walkway. Admiring the artwork decorating the halls, they made their way to the correct elevator and rode it up to the sixth floor. Janella's eyes grew wide as they walked down the hall of the neurology ward. There were people with bandages around their heads, others walking with nurses who helped them stay upright with a sturdy belt slung under their armpits, and multiple wheelchair patients.

When they got to Dorine Carmine's room, the door was just being opened by an aide carrying a large plastic sack. A faint odor caught Gretchen's attention briefly, letting her know what was in the bag. Mrs. Carmine was propped up in bed with her eyes closed and one arm tucked down by her side.

The three tiptoed in quietly, each finding a seat in the good-sized room. Janella and Gretchen sat in chairs at the foot of the bed, while Ethel sat close to her friend beside the bed. After about ten minutes, Dorine opened her eyes and noticed Ethel sitting next to her.

"Oh, Ettil, good to see oo!" Dorine's smile was more even than it had been the last time they had seen her, and her speech – though far from perfect – seemed to have improved also. She looked around and saw the other two. "Hi, Getchen. Hoo is wit you?"

"This is one of my students," replied Gretchen. "She's visiting us over the Thanksgiving Holiday."

"Tat's nice," said Mrs. Carmine. "Tangsgiving! Oh, my! You are botherin wit me on Tangsgiving?"

"We want to be here!" declared Ethel firmly.

But her friend wasn't convinced. "Oo should be ome wit your famly."

"We are where we want to be." Janella confirmed Ethel's answer with a big smile. "You don't know how miserable my holiday could have been."

Mrs. Carmine almost glared at her as she said, "Not as mizerbal as mine!"

"Oh, but you have many things to be thankful for," commented Gretchen in a neutral tone, hoping to give Dorine's thoughts a more positive direction. "We found you quickly, so you got the medicine that helps stroke victims recover quickly. You are already showing signs of improvement from the last time we saw you, and while you are recovering you are in one of the best hospitals around."

"You are tryin' to cheer me up."

"I am."

"Well, I rather talk to Etel!" Mrs. Carmine sounded fierce, but smiled again as she turned to her friend.

Janella raised her eyebrows as she looked at her teacher. Gretchen murmured, "It's better that she has the strength to be fussy, than to just feel sorry for herself."

Janella nodded her understanding. They let the two friends visit until a nurse came in to help her patient order supper. Janella leaned over to Gretchen and whispered, "That was a strange conversation. Your mom had to have everything explained twice and your neighbor kept using words that you would have told me were 'inappropriate.'"

Gretchen chuckled softly. "That's the damage of the stroke. I've never heard Mrs. Carmine use those words before."

After the nurse left, Ethel and her friend chatted a little longer, and then Dorine leaned back against her pillows and closed her eyes.

Gretchen got up. "I think that is our cue to go get our supper."

The three made their way down to the hospital cafeteria. Gretchen and her mother got the Chinese special, but Janella picked collard greens and a pulled pork sandwich.

"That's an interesting choice for a teenager," commented Gretchen.

"Well, I've been thinking a lot about my Grandma today." Janella replied with a smile. "This is a meal she would serve."

Gretchen nodded as she selected her utensils. She paid for everyone's food, and they found a quiet table looking out on one of the hospital entrances.

Ethel was quiet, concentrating on her food. After a few minutes, Gretchen turned to Janella who was sitting beside her. "Is it as good as your grandmother's?"

Janella shook her head. "The barbecue isn't quite right on the pork, but it is still good."

Gretchen nodded. "Your grandmother sounds like a good cook."

Janella swallowed a bite. "Yes, but she's an even better person. Better than my mom."

Gretchen schooled her face to not react to that statement. She waited for the girl to continue, which she did after her next bite.

"When my dad was killed – it was a case of mistaken identity – he was mistaken for a gang-banger – Grandma visited the shooter in prison. More than once."

"Why?" asked Ethel.

"Oh, she figured no one needed saving more than the young man who murdered her son." Janella took another bite and chewed. After swallowing, she continued again. "The first time she went she never even got to see him, but she could hear him swearing as he shouted that he didn't want to see her. Still, she kept going back until he finally gave in and decided to swear to her face. She just grinned and said that he should be thankful that she didn't have some soap."

Gretchen chuckled. "Your grandma sounds like quite a lady."

"Yup... but my mom couldn't understand where Grandma was coming from. She wanted to personally tear out the heart of the murderer."

"Hummm."

Janella gave something between a laugh and a snort. "Grandma came closer to getting her hands on his heart than my mom did, and without getting in trouble with the law herself."

Ethel looked over at Janella in admiration. "You are a wise young lady!"

Gretchen nodded. "I agree."

Janella sighed deeply. "I'm glad someone thinks so."

Later that night in the hotel, Gretchen lay awake as the other two slept. Her mind flitted through the events of the last few days. Tying Mrs. Carmine to a chair. Finding Janella sleeping on her couch. Sending her husband off to Kansas City. If the trip had been a few months ago, she would have been going along, but now she had one - no, two - no, in some ways, three - precious souls to watch over.

Would she have had what it takes to visit the person who murdered one of her family? She looked forward to meeting Janella's grandma. Almost certainly she would like her. She had expressed some of those feelings to Ben in a call from Kansas City. Now, she tried to form her jumbled thoughts into a prayer, and that did it. She fell asleep.

The next morning, after breakfast at the hotel, they returned to the hospital about 9:30. They had spent a couple of hours with Dorine Carmine and had just left her room, when a police officer stopped in front of them.

As the officer said, "Ma'am, may I speak." Janella bolted.

As she sprinted down the hospital hall, Janella shouted over her shoulder, "I am not going back! I am not going to live with that man!"

"Janella! Come back!" Gretchen couldn't think of anything else to say.

The officer automatically took off after her, catching up with her as they left the Neurology unit. By then he had thought through what was happening enough not to tackle the girl. When she saw him, Janella did a 180 and ran the opposite direction. The office stopped and called, "I'm not here to take you anywhere, miss."

Janella's change of direction brought her right back to where Gretchen was standing at the entrance to the Neurology unit. "Please. stop, Janella. I'll protect you!"

The officer was shouting, "I am here only to deliver a message. Please, listen!"

Janella paused. Ahead she saw some men that she was pretty sure were hospital security. Behind Gretchen a couple of large male nurses approached. Behind the officer a group of people had gathered, incidentally blocking the hall more completely than the officer alone.

Gretchen tentatively reached for Janella's hand. "Let's see what the policeman has to say. He says he's just got a message."

Janella stood, panting. She glanced around one more time, realizing how much attention she was getting.

"Let's go into the Neuro waiting room," suggested Gretchen. Janella nodded.

Gretchen nodded to the security people and the male nurses and they fell back. She saw the police officer dispersing the crowd down the hall.

In the waiting room, Janella restlessly plopped into a lounge chair. Gretchen picked a chair close to her, and closer to the room's door than Janella's chair. One of the female nurses appeared at the door with Ethel. Gretchen motioned for her to come in. Ethel picked a chair on the other side of the girl and reached for her hand.

The officer appeared in the doorway. "Is it okay for me to come in?" he asked.

The older women looked at Janella. She made a face, but nodded.

The officer entered the room slowly and came just a few steps past the entrance and stopped. "I was told to come here to Neurology to find Mrs. Gretchen Parks."

"I am Mrs. Parks", replied Gretchen.

"I wasn't told -- why I was coming to Neurology. Are all of you all right?"

"Yes -- I mean, no -- but the three of us are. Janella has obviously had a lot to handle recently, but we're here to see a friend."

The policeman lifted an eyebrow, but nodded. "I was going to ask to see you, Mrs. Parks, privately. However, under the circumstances I think it is best if I give the message to you all." He paused. "May I first ask a question?"

The three nodded, glancing at each other as they did so.

The officer continued. "Young lady, the man you were so determined not to live with -- was his name Jeremy Munch?"

Janella nodded.

The officer gazed intently at her. "I'm sorry, but I need a moment." He saw Janella's alarmed expression and hurriedly assured her, "It's not to arrange taking you anywhere." He smiled briefly and nodded as he exited the room.

He was back a moment later and took up his position three steps inside the door. He cleared his throat.

Gretchen found herself gripping the arms of her chair.

"At the suggestion of --" he referred to a paper in his hand, "Reverend Parks ---"

"My husband," Gretchen inserted for clarification.

The officer nodded. "At the suggestion of Reverend Parks the sheriff's department of Des Moines County, Iowa, drove to the residence of Mr. Munch several times in the last couple of days. The first two times, when they went to the door, there was no response to their knocks. The third time, there appeared to be a party going on."

The officer cleared her throat again. "There were many cars parked around the area and the deputy decided not to stop -- at least not without backup."

Gretchen lifted her eyebrows.

"The house was out in the country, a remote location. The first turn back toward the main road was almost a mile away, so the house was visible in the rear mirror of the police car for quite a ways."

Gretchen nodded her understanding again.

"When the officer reached the turn, he stopped to report in. It was then that he heard -- and felt -- a sound that he could not immediately identify. He looked back toward the house with the party only to see a fireball."

Gretchen gasped.

The expression on the officer's face was grim. "Returning, the officer arrived at the house to find a few people crying or screaming outside. A few lay dead or injured on the ground. Not much was left of the house." He paused as he rubbed his forehead. "Investigation is not complete, but they are pretty sure Mr. Munch was in the house."

Gretchen let her breath out slowly.

"So my stepdad's meth lab blew up," Janella said in a flat voice.

As the officer nodded, a lady wearing a clerical collar appeared at the door.

After glancing her way, the officer said, "I hope you don't mind. When I stepped out a while ago, I asked that a hospital chaplain come. I can't stay long, and I thought it might be helpful to have someone to talk to about this situation."

Their stop at the Herbert Hoover Presidential museum was muted by the news that they had received from the police officer. Janella had confessed to the chaplain that she had repeatedly wished her stepfather dead, and the chaplain reassured her that wishing it had not caused it -- that Janella was not responsible for Mr. Munch's death. Gretchen knew that the girl would still need help getting past feelings of both guilt and relief. Gretchen herself was just stunned. Ethel felt the undercurrent of feelings, rather than remembering the details; and she was tired and off schedule.

Though it was cold and snow still covered the ground, the Herbert Hoover museum remained open. They turned into an almost empty parking lot, went inside, and dropped money in the donation box, before entering the exhibit area. Gretchen had been there before, but neither of the others had. They walked through exhibits on Hoover's education at Stanford, his years as a mining engineer in China, his work feeding the starving of Europe after World War I, and his acceptance of a presidential cabinet post.

Ethel shook her head as she read that the presidency had been Hoover's first elected office. "No wonder he had problems," she stated simply.

"Yea," said Janella, "He thought a bunch of greedy spoiled people would, out of the goodness of their hearts, help others and 'do the right thing.'"

"That's an interesting way to put it," murmured Gretchen. "He certainly was more successful at doing what he wanted to do -- help others -- when he could leave politics out of it".

Janella turned to look at her teacher. "Why did the Great Depression happen anyway? What do stocks in a company have to do with people going hungry?"

Gretchen thought for a minute, rubbing the spots on her arm which seemed better today; and while she was thinking Ethel spoke up. "It's fear. The connection is fear. If people had not panicked, things would not have gotten as bad as they did. Fear is still our enemy."

Gretchen nodded. "Mom's right. People had been living in prosperity, but a prosperity not based on real economic progress, but on -- on creative bookkeeping. When the bubble burst, rich people weren't prepared to face the hardship caused by their own greed and manipulation. They wanted an easy out --"

"So they jumped out of windows," added Janella grimly.

Gretchen grimaced. "Some did. Others made decisions that created more problems. Some of those decisions were Hoover's -- he got some terrible advice from his people. But the ideas which had helped feed soldiers during WWI, and Europeans after the war, didn't work in this situation. People weren't willing to be sacrificially generous to get their neighbors out of trouble."

"The roaring twenties hadn't helped the character of the American people," added Ethel.

Janella closed her eyes in thought. "Do you mean that being rich and comfortable made people more selfish and -- and scared?"

Gretchen sighed as they put on their coats and headed back toward the car.

It was Ethel again who responded, "When has being rich made someone a better person?"

All were silent until seat belts were fastened, then Janella murmured, "Being rich certainly didn't make my stepdad better. He let my mom go to prison for what he did." After another moment of silence she added, "Of course, Mom wanted to be rich too. She was stupid to ever go with him. She knew what he was."

Gretchen looked expectantly at her mom for more words of wisdom, but Ethel was staring blankly ahead. *Poor Mom; she's reached her limit,* thought Gretchen. *She worked so hard to be there for her friend, and to make it through the museum that...* She glanced back over at her mother. Ethel's eyes were already closed and her head drooping.

Gretchen thought a moment, but wasn't coming up with a good response to Janella's words. She glanced back at her student and discovered that the girl was sleeping, too. For a moment Gretchen missed Ben very much, then she put her feelings aside and concentrated on watching the traffic on busy highway 80.

Later that evening she was in bed hugging Ben's pillow when he called. "How is everyone?" were his first words.

"Ben, do you know that we were visited by a police officer at the hospital this morning?"

There was the sound of Ben clearing his throat. "Yes, I did. They called my cell. That's how they knew where to look for you."

"I wondered." She blew her breath through closed teeth. "It's been quite an emotional day. I'm afraid I kept the television off when we got home. I didn't think it would help any of us to hear news reports about the explosion which destroyed Janella's home of the last year and a half."

"That was wise," replied Ben. "My news isn't quite as earth-shaking, but it was an emotional day here, too."

"I'm tired, but not ready to sleep, so you might as well give me the blow-by-blow about what is going on in Kansas City."

Gretchen thought she heard the sound of a chuckle. "Can you switch emotional gears for a while?" Ben responded.

"It would probably be a relief."

"We had two types of tasks to accomplish today, some general repair work and walking the streets in search of hungry street people." Ben sighed. "We had plenty of volunteers for plaster and painting work, not so many for the other. So -- I volunteered to go with the pastor."

"So you got to work with Pastor Manuel today."

"Yes. He is certainly a sincere Christian -- and an interesting personality."

"He seemed so to me."

"Yes, and tough. Gretchen, it's the end of November and definitely chilly. Just skiffs of snow on the ground in K.C., but the temperature hovered around freezing."

"Uh-huh."

"I had my coat, gloves, and hat, but no long johns and I got cold!"

"Oh, my!"

"But by the end of our hike -- because that was what it was, a fast-paced hike, with intermittent stops to stand in the wind on the cold cement sidewalks to talk to people. I got colder and colder."

"Are you feeling all right now?"

Ben gave a laugh. "I think so. But Manuel just kept going. Nothing seemed to phase him. He'd brought a sack full of gloves and scarves, but when he had passed them all out, he gave one man the gloves he wore. Then he just stuffed his hands in his pockets between stops."

"That does show dedication."

"Humm, yes. Then we came across another homeless person -- a middle-aged woman."

"And you gave her your gloves."

Ben sighed. "You got it."

"I'm proud of you."

"Thanks, I'm not. My actions were right, but my attitude was anything but."

Gretchen laughed.

"I'm serious, Gretchen!"

"Oh, I know you are, and I know attitude is important, but you still did the right thing."

"But they were my special leather gloves you gave me last Christmas!"

"I guess I'll just have to by you the cheaper gloves-by-the-dozen so you have more to give away. And you can give them without regrets."

Ben groaned.

"Ben."

"Yes."

"Ask God to give you the -- the persuasive abilities to get someone else to go out tomorrow."

"Don't worry, I will!"

CHAPTER 11

Gretchen was just drifting off to sleep after that phone call when she heard a commotion downstairs. As the sounds got louder, she forced herself to wake up, pull on her robe, and head down the stairs.

Ethel was standing in the middle of the living room, shifting her weight from one foot to the other. Janella stood next to her, holding one hand. "It's okay, Grandma Ethel. We are at home. There's your bed right over there."

"This isn't my home," whined Ethel. "I don't know this place. I live on a farm. Where's my husband?"

Gretchen deliberately made some noise. Janella looked up, turning Ethel toward the stairs. Gretchen smiled, though she did not feel happy at the moment, and spoke. "Hi, Mom. Hi, Janella. What's up?"

"Is that you, Gretchen?"

"It's me, Mom. This is my house, and you've come to stay with me."

"Oh – yes – uh – I did." Ethel looked around.

Janella patted Ethel's arm. "Things look different in the middle of the night, Grandma Ethel. It's okay."

Gretchen made it the rest of the way down the stairs and put her arm around her mother's shoulders. "Let me help you back to bed, Mom."

Ethel allowed herself to be guided back to her bed. As Gretchen covered her back up, she asked, "Was I dreaming?"

Gretchen shrugged. "I don't know, Mom. I do know that sometimes I'm a little disoriented when I first wake up. And it's more likely to happen after a long hard day."

"I had a long hard day?"

"We all did, Mom. We all did."

Janella had turned on the television while they were talking. She was punching buttons Gretchen normally didn't use and she had a screen of internet options showing. "Grandma Ethel, what is your favorite quiet music?" Janella shifted her gaze to Gretchen when Ethel just looked confused. "Mrs. P, I thought I'd play some relaxing music. What do you think your mom would like?"

Gretchen frowned in thought for a moment. She understood what Janella was trying to do, but she was old-school enough to think in terms of a CD player when she thought about listening to music. "Quiet music – let's see – Mom used to play hymns or – or Pachelbel's Canon after we went to bed."

Janella nodded and turned back to her work with the remote and the television. Soon an image of a peaceful country scene appeared and the opening strains of the well-known classical piece played softly. Janella whispered, "I found a forty-five minute version."

"Thank you, Janella," Gretchen whispered back. She sat beside her mother until Ethel's breathing became slow and regular, then she transferred her position next to Janella on the sofa. Janella smiled sleepily up at her. Gretchen patted the girl's shoulder, then reached up to put her hand over a spot on her neck that had begun to itch. Janella closed her eyes. Gretchen patted her shoulder again, then got up to return to her own bed.

Between her thoughts about the day, the night, and the welt that was swelling on her neck, Gretchen had problems getting to sleep, in spite of the tiring day. The next day, all three slept in. By the time Gretchen made it downstairs again, her mother and Janella were sitting at the kitchen table drinking coffee. Gretchen raised an eyebrow as she looked at Janella's mug, but didn't say anything.

In a very parental style, Janella turned to Ethel and said, "There's your daughter now! You just sit here and continue drinking your coffee; I've got to talk to Mrs. – to Gre – to her for a moment." She patted Ethel's hand and continued, "I'll be back soon."

Gretchen suppressed a smile as Janella approached her, motioning for them to both go to the living room. Gretchen turned to walk with her and Janella leaned close and murmured. "Grandma Ethel was a little confused when she first woke up, but she seems fine now. I made her coffee."

"You made her coffee?"

Janella looked slightly flustered. "Sure. I used a coffee filter and made individual cups in the microwave."

"Microwave? Do you not know how to use the coffee maker?"

Janella flushed slightly. "I do, Mrs. Parks, but you hadn't given me permission to use it, so I did it the way I'd figured out on my own living with – with --" The memory of what had happened to her stepfather came flooding back and Janella drooped.

So much for the parent attitude, thought Gretchen. Out loud she said, "The way you made the coffee sounds very much like the traditional Costa Rican way, except they use a cloth filter."

Janella perked up. "I think it was Costa Rican coffee. I used those little packets from the hotel we stayed in in Iowa City."

Gretchen's eyebrow raised again as she wondered what else Janella might have taken from the hotel.

Janella seemed to read her mind. "It is okay to take those isn't it? Those and the little shampoos? Grandma sometimes took those. I know not to take towels. You get charged for them."

Gretchen willed her eyebrow back to its proper level and turned the corners of her mouth up. "Yes, it's fine. I would feel a little more comfortable if you had checked with me before you took them. Just so I knew what you were doing."

Janella looked away, her eyes sparkling with tears. "I'm sorry. I've just gotten so used to sneaking around Jeremy. I forget I don't have to sneak with you, Mrs. Parks." There was a short sound between a choke and a sob at the end of Janella's words.

Gretchen's eyes filled with tears, too, as she took Janella in her arms. "Oh, dear girl, you have been through so much!"

Janella buried her face in Gretchen's shoulder and sobbed.

After a minute Gretchen reached for some tissues, and, while Janella used them vigorously on her eyes and nose, Gretchen asked, "Was there something else you wanted to talk with me about, Janella?"

Janella looked up from a tissue.

"You acted like you wanted to talk to me alone about something..."

Janella blew her nose once more. "Yes, there was." She didn't look quite as parental now with red eyes, but her shoulders squared and chin went up. "Twice while I have been here, your mom has been up and – and not making a whole lot of sense – in the middle of the night. Did this happen before?"

"Not that I know of. Not since she got settled in here."

Janella nodded wisely. "But any upset and it affects Grandma Ethel big time."

It was Gretchen's turn to nod.

"What do you plan on doing after I'm gone? Who will watch over her in the middle of the night?"

Now Gretchen sighed. "Those are good questions, Janella. Until our neighbor's stroke, things seemed to be stabilizing. We were hopeful that Mom would be safe here. Now – I agree with you – that safety is in question."

"What are you going to do?"

"I really don't know." Gretchen paused, thinking. "Your grandma won't be coming for a few days. I think this problem is not one that can be solved instantaneously. I need to do some serious thinking, talk to my husband Ben, and --"

"And pray!" declared Janella.

Gretchen looked at her in surprise. "Yes, pray; but I didn't expect you to say that."

"It's what Grandma Kelly would do."

Gretchen nodded slowly. "I am going to like meeting her. She is my kind of lady."

Janella's eyes danced. "She sure is."

The rest of the day Gretchen kept her charges busy with ordinary things, her thoughts often straying to wondering what Ben was doing. Ben kept busy with drywall and sandpaper and paint. He had prayed the night before that God would provide a replacement for him with Brother Manuel, and that He would do it in a way that was definitely a God-thing.

Ben's sleeping bag was next to Moses Martin, the most conservative of the people on the trip. As they were getting ready for bed, Ben mentioned how extraordinary it was to spend the day with a man who took the Bible seriously and lived so completely what he believed. At breakfast the next morning he ended up sitting next to a man so liberal that Ben had difficulty thinking of him as a Christian.

"Hello, Ted, did you sleep well?"

"Ha! As well as can be expected on the floor. If I didn't so strongly believe in James 2:18, I wouldn't have come here."

"I'll show you my faith by my works?"

"Yes, that's the verse."

"Well, the repair work *is* good work, but we aren't *showing* it to anyone," Ben found himself saying, he wasn't sure why. "Yesterday I gave my good gloves to a homeless woman. I didn't want to, but I did. She got to see my faith by my works. Others got to see Brother Manuel's. He handed out over a dozen pair. He puts all of us to shame."

The other man was quiet through breakfast and disappeared for a while afterwards. While Ted was gone, Ben saw Moses Martin approach Brother Manuel. He couldn't hear the conversation, but he saw the nod and slap on the back by Manuel and figured Moses had volunteered for today's homeless hike. He was getting sandpaper out to smooth splinters in old wood when he saw Ted Jones again. Ted was holding a plastic store bag as he approached Brother Martin. Pulling out gloves and then socks, Ted was obviously asking to accompany the street preacher on his rounds. Again there was a nod and a slap on the back. Ben bit his lip to keep from laughing. He almost wished he was going along to see how the liberal and conservative men worked together today.

Two vans had traveled together to Kansas City, but, because of Sunday obligations, one van was returning late on Saturday night. The other would follow the next day after worshiping with Manuel's congregation. Because of Ben's vacations earlier in the year, he needed to return. It turned out Ted Jones and

Moses Martin were also going back in the first van.

Ben curled up in the back seat and tried to sleep, but it was hard. Ted told the story of every pair of gloves he had handed out and every pair of socks. Ben caught the note of pride in the man's voice and thought of a Bible verse: "But Jesus said, Forbid him not: for there is no man which shall do a miracle in my name, that can lightly speak evil of me."[Mark 9:39] Maybe handing out gloves wasn't actually a miracle, but Ben thought the same principle applied.

Finally, Ted finished his recital and Ben thought he would have some peace and quiet to rest. However, Moses Martin now started to talk. It seems that Ted's purchases had inspired Moses to stop at a Cheep-O store and stock up on knit hats and scarves which he passed out to the homeless who already had gloves and socks.

Moses droned on as long as Ted had, but Ben was tired enough that he drifted off to sleep eventually. Before he did, he remembered Brother Manuel's aside to him in parting, another scripture: "...whether in pretense, or in truth, Christ is preached; and I therein do rejoice, yea, and will rejoice."[Philippians 1:18] The man who did so well at helping and encouraging the downtrodden, also understood and encouraged those whose motives for joining the cause were less than perfect.

One of the men in this van lived just ten miles from Ben, and Ben was grateful that he was willing to go out of his way to deliver him to his door. He did not check the clock as he tiptoed past Ethel and Janella downstairs. He figured it would just depress him to know how little of the night was left. Gretchen stirred as he snuggled in next to her. She threw an arm around him and mumbled something which was probably meant to be a welcome.

CHAPTER 12

Morning was more hectic that Ben liked; Gretchen had allowed him to sleep longer than usual. Even though the ladies made sure things were ready for him when he descended the stairs, he felt "off." He tried to take time alone with the Lord, but the memories of his trip and the noises from downstairs kept interrupting his concentration. "Forgive me, Lord," Ben prayed. "This service will start the church's preparation for the celebration of your birth, and I am not at my best. Please, help me."

The Sunday School hour ended uneventfully, and everyone moved to the sanctuary of the country church for the main worship service. A couple of the youth played and sang modern choruses to open the service, then old Mrs. Peabody assumed her place at the organ. Ben marveled at her. She was almost never sick, still played very well, but appeared to sleep through most of his sermons. He knew that when she could no longer play, they would probably have to do without an organist; there were no replacements available.

They formally opened the service with "Now Thank We All Our God," a good Thanksgiving hymn. After that, a trustee had a few announcements and so did the Christian Education board. Next came the greeting time, a favorite in this close family church. Ben watched people cross aisles to greet each other. Even Ethel and Janella were getting into the spirit of the greetings as they sat close to the front with Gretchen.

Just as the congregation was returning to their seats, the doors opened in the back and two late-comers entered. Ben noticed that his greeters were still on duty and helped the two find seats in the next-to-back row. What caught his eye was that the two were strangers, and that they were African

American.

The man was the darkest skinned person in attendance this morning; the lady was about the same color as many of the "white" farmers who lived their lives in the sun. The people around them were welcoming; Ben was glad. When the Calhoun boy had brought a Korean bride back from his military tour in Asia, there had been a few in this very white neighborhood who had not been so welcoming. Ben had preached a series of pointed sermons on the mixed marriages in the Old Testament, the deacons had talked to the offenders, and all had settled down.

He nodded at the middle-aged couple, but did not call attention to them. Somehow the woman seemed strangely familiar, though he couldn't think why. From the pulpit it was hard to get a detailed look at either of their features. Had someone followed him home from Kansas City? But these were not street people.

Ben had entitled his sermon of the week: Thankful Service. He used scriptures talking about a spirit of thankfulness for what God has done for us. After introducing the Biblical information, he talked a little about his experiences in Kansas City over the last few days. Getting a sudden inspiration, he asked Gretchen to come up and tell about the service she had experienced at Brother Manuel's church.

She shared about the greeters with food sacks, and the arrangement of old living room furniture mixed with folding chairs. She was just starting to tell about the street person who had gotten up and rearranged the furniture so she would have the best seat, when she saw the visiting couple. Ben saw her give a gasp as if she recognized them. Then she smoothly finished what she was going to say.

She glanced once more at the couple, and then at Janella, before sitting down. Light began to dawn on him.

Ben moved to the back of the church to give the benediction, not his usual practice, but he wanted to be in position to greet their guests. He turned to them, shook the hand of the man, welcoming him. Then, turning to the woman, he found himself staring at striking hazel eyes. "Glad to meet you, Mrs. Kelly," he said.

Grandma Kelly gave a short laugh. "It's the eyes, isn't it? I can never get away with pretending I'm not Janella's relation."

"And there would be no reason to not want to claim her," remarked Gretchen as she approached.

"No, there is not," said Mrs. Kelly with certainty. "I have a wonderful granddaughter."

Just then Janella reached the group, leading Ethel gently. Gretchen replaced Janella's guiding hand with her own, freeing Janella to rush into her grandmother's arms.

"Oh, baby girl! My sweet baby girl," crooned her grandma. "You have been having such a rough time, and I couldn't find you – though I certainly tried."

CHAPTER 13

Gretchen and Ben didn't put up their Christmas tree until the week before Christmas. There had been too many things happening.

The Kellys allowed Janella to stay the week after Thanksgiving to finish things up at school. During that time they visited her mother in prison and investigated the situation surrounding the explosion at the house she had been living in.

Dorine was moved from the University of Iowa Hospital to a rehabilitation center in Burlington. She'd selected Burlington, because a niece worked at a senior living center there. The hospital had strongly suggested that she prepare to go into a care center, at least for the winter. So, she had reserved a room there, as soon as the rehab center released her. She was already able to move herself in a wheelchair, but needed to be able to transfer herself before she would be accepted in an assisted living facility.

Several days after her friend had made her move to Burlington, Ethel folded her napkin after supper and looked seriously at her daughter and son-in-law. "We have to talk," she said.

Gretchen's mouth dropped open, but she quickly closed it.

Ben handled the statement with less surprise. "What do we need to talk about, Mom Gunther?"

Ethel licked her lips as she tried to figure out how to start. "Right now --" she chuckled, "I'd better finish this before I space out again – I know that I am often confused and this makes it hard for you to care for me without making difficulties for your other responsibilities." She chuckled again. "And, you will have to admit, that my living arrangements here are rather haphazard. Not exactly designed for an old lady."

"Mom, we --"

Ethel waved her hand to silence her daughter. "I know you've done your best for the time being, and that you would be willing to do much more." She sighed. "I like being close to you, but life is getting scarier, and I need a place that is as safe as possible. You need me to be in that kind of place, too."

This time Gretchen and Ben were both quiet as Gretchen's mother gathered her thoughts again. She turned to Ben. "I would like you to take me to the Sunnybreeze Assisted Living tomorrow to see if I can get a room there. That's where my friend – uh – my friend is planning on going."

"Mom, are you sure?" asked Gretchen.

Ethel laughed again. "I'm not sure of much these days. That is why I'm pretty sure that I should go to Sunny – that place." She noticed a frown on Ben's face. "If you're wondering how we're going to pay for this, I can show you if we can get to my old dresser."

"Well, let's go into your room and see what you've got in your dresser," replied Ben as he moved in the direction of their converted dining room.

Ethel shook her head. "Not that dresser. The old one."

"The old one?" questioned Gretchen. "What do you mean?"

"The old one we brought from the farm and had by the back door of our apartment."

Gretchen frowned. "The one that looked more like it belonged in the barn?"

Ethel started to look worried. "Yes, that one."

Gretchen took a deep breath. "Mom, I gave that to your neighbor in Kansas City."

Ethel's brow relaxed. "Well, that's inconvenient, but not as bad as if you had thrown it away. Just contact her and tell her that there are some papers we need from it."

Gretchen whipped out her phone and chose the right contact.

"Hull-o, Mrs. Parks," answered Sylvia, "Long time."

"Sylvia, Do you still have that old dresser?"

"I do Mrs. P. Do you want it back?"

"I'm not sure... Mom says there are some papers in it that she needs."

"I haven't seen any papers. Are they hidden underneath or something?"

"I'm not sure... I'll put Mom on." Gretchen held out the phone for Ethel.

Taking the phone, Ethel asked, "Who am I talking to now?"

Gretchen started. Her mother had been so focused a few minutes ago; apparently she had reached her limit, or was close to it. "It is your neighbor Sylvia."

"Okay. Hi, Sylvia, what do you want?" began Ethel.

"Hi, my old neighbor. You say there is something in the old dresser you need."

"I did?"

"Yes."

"Hmm. Then it must be hidden somewhere."

"Do you remember where?"

A light flickered in Ethel's eyes. "It's a puzzle. Grandpa made the dresser a puzzle."

"How do I do this puzzle, friend?"

The light faded from Ethel's eyes. Her shoulders slumped. "Would you say that again?"

"How do I do this puzzle dresser?"

Ethel shook her head. "I don't remember. I'm sorry, I don't remember."

Ben motioned for the phone. "Sylvia, this is Ben. Ethel was telling us that she had something that would help pay for a room in a senior living place..."

"Yes, yes!" declared Ethel. "in – in – stocks."

"She says, stocks, or some kind of investment," said Ben.

"But that doesn't tell me how to find it."

"I know, Sylvia. The only thing I can think of is to call you back when Mom remembers."

"Guess so... though I will investigate the dresser in my spare time."

Ben and Gretchen, at Ethel's insistence, took her to the senior living facility the next day, and they began the paperwork. There were two of the smaller rooms available next to each other. As Ben wrote a personal check for the down payment on Ethel's room, he asked what it would take to hold the other room for her friend. The manager smiled. "It's already taken care of."

Sylvia still had not figured out the puzzle of the dresser by the time that they moved Ethel into Sunnybreeze. The next day, at the somewhat confused urging of Ethel, Ben and Gretchen drove to Kansas City.

This visit was different from the last two. Ethel's former apartment had been rented to a single mom with 2 kids. Brother Manuel was out of town at a conference. Since the Parks weren't sure that Sylvia would feel comfortable with them crowding into her place, they found a hotel room close to the local university. That also gave them some time to themselves.

They texted Sylvia when they arrived, but she returned the text, saying she had been called in to cover someone else's shift. They were welcome to stop by for a key and work on the dresser, but they said that they would just wait until the next day.

"I've been so curious. Don't want to wait long. Come over in the morning asap."

"Will do. Prob about 9."

":-)"

The next morning Ben and Gretchen arrived at Sylvia's promptly at 9:00 a.m. She took them right to the spot in the laundry room where she had put the dresser. It had been pulled out from the wall earlier, as Sylvia had attempted to find the secret of the furniture.

"I've thumped on it and measured it," Sylvia explained, "and I'm pretty sure that at least part of the back is hollow... but I haven't found out how to get into the hollow place without tearing it up."

By the time Sylvia had finished saying this, Ben was doing his own thumping. "Yes, the back sounds hollow, but dresser backs are usually so thin they would sound hollow." He took out a tape measure and pulled out a drawer. "Distance to back from the inside," he murmured. He moved to the outside wall. "Distance to back on the outside... About two inches more!"

He turned to Gretchen. "Sylvia's right! Now how do we get in there?"

Gretchen moved to the dresser and started feeling various sections of wood. One corner seemed a little loose, but it would not move more than an eighth of an inch. There was a nob in the front center, just under the top, which turned, but seemed to do nothing when it was turned.

She started pulling out each drawer and feeling around inside. After a bit, she stuck her head inside. Sylvia stuck a flashlight in Gretchen's hand, and she started moving it around. She reached up and pulled on a loose board right behind the turning knob. Nothing. She pulled the nob straight out, and the board dropped down. In fact, a shallow box dropped to the bottom of the dresser. Inside the box were a few papers.

Ben and Gretchen looked them over eagerly, but found only records of a few bank cds.

"We don't even know if these are still valid," murmured Ben.

"And there isn't nearly enough here to make much difference in long-term care," added Gretchen.

Ben raised an eyebrow. "Remember Mom's mental state. She may not have as much as she remembered."

Gretchen sighed and started to speak, but Ben hushed her. "We will see that your mom gets the care she needs. Even if I have to find some part-time work."

Gretchen smiled and picked up one of the top drawers to return it to its regular place in the dresser. Somehow it wasn't going in all the way. She pulled it out, put it back in, and tried to close the drawer again. Still, it would not go in more than two-thirds of the way.

Silvia started bouncing. "Oh! Is there more puzzle?"

Ben bent down in front of the dresser. He pulled the drawer out a little and reached under and behind it. There was a thud. He pulled the little drawer all the way out and then reached back in. Another tug, and a creak sounded from the back of the dresser. Gretchen bent the top of the back board back and forth, but couldn't get it to really open.

Ben dropped all the way to his knees and studied the bottom of the dresser. Half way back, another board protruded above the base. He gave it a yank. As he did so, the whole back dropped with a whoosh to the floor and papers followed, like oversized confetti on New Year's Eve.

Gretchen dropped to the floor now, too. So did Sylvia. Together the three organized stocks, bonds, and more certificates of deposit.

Ben's voice trembled. "I think we've found what they did with the money from the sale of their farm."

Silvia clapped her hands in delight. "Ethel will have enough to be cared for royally!"

"Well, we don't really know how much these are worth now," cautioned Ben. "But it does appear we'll have significant help."

"Do you want the dresser back?" asked Sylvia.

Gretchen looked at the piece longingly for a second, then squared her shoulders. "I gave it to you. It's yours. And there are safer ways to store your assets."

"Yes," said Ben. "A fire could have been devastating."

"And memory loss almost was," added Gretchen.

Now, just a week before Christmas, Ben had been in contact with his financial adviser about what they had found, and things were set up for Ethel to receive a regular income from the investments. They were also helping Dorine's sister get her room ready at the care center, because Dorine was improving rapidly.

Gretchen put one more ornament on the tree and rubbed a new red spot on her arm. The itching was a distraction, but nothing was going to keep her from being thankful for how well things were working out for her mother – and how they had worked out for Janella.

CHAPTER 14

"Christmas may seem almost anticlimactic," Ben commented as he finished wrapping a present on the kitchen table.

"What do you mean?" asked Gretchen, pausing to hold her hand over a group of welts on one arm. "Our daughter's family will be down for a couple of days, and Cal is flying up."

"But how does that compare to mission trips, helping neighbors with strokes, and students with life-trauma?"

Gretchen shrugged. "I guess we'll see… I just wish I could figure out how to get rid of this rash, or whatever it is."

The rest of the day both Gretchen and Ben did little things to prepare for the Christmas celebration and the visit from their children. That evening, Gretchen applied the steroid cream shes had been given by her doctor as she got ready for bed. Ben led their evening prayers, and they settled down to sleep.

In the middle of the night, Gretchen stirred, waking enough to consider getting up to go to the bathroom. A stray tickle on her neck automatically brought up her hand to scratch it. There was something more than skin under the finger which touched her neck. And that something was moving.

Immediately, Gretchen was wide awake. She clasped the small thing from her neck between two fingers. Slipping out of bed, she hurried to the bathroom and turned on a light. Afraid that opening her fingers would cause her to loose what she held, she turned and scurried down to the kitchen where she got out a small plastic baggie. She dropped what she held into the bag and quickly sealed it. It was a bug. Gretchen, thinking about where she had been when she found it, figured it probably was a bedbug. Her skin crawled. And itched.

The next day, after talking to an exterminator, who told

her that women are more likely to be bothered by the bugs than men, Gretchen spent her day feeding everything washable through her washing machine; and, those things which were fabric, but not washable, were mercilessly thrown in the drier to be exposed to bug-killing heat.

A roll of garbage bags stood on the table to receive the treated clothes, and Ben stood by to take everything they wouldn't need in the next week out to the garage. While he waited, he was making phone calls.

"Hello, Cal, be sure to pack your swim trunks," said Ben.

"Dad? Swim trunks for Illinois in December?"

"We're celebrating Christmas at a motel, Cal. We are experiencing – ah – bedbugs."

"In your house?"

"In our house. Yes. Pack your trunks."

Cal laughed. "Dad, we don't seem to be doing anything normally this year."

"With that I agree, son. See you soon. I've got to call your sister now."

When the exterminator came to treat their house the first time, he encouraged them by saying the only signs of bedbugs were in their bed and the living room couch. When he came for the second round of treatments, he told them they would probably never know for sure where they picked them up. Hotels were a common culprit. Schools were another possibility. The good news was that bedbugs did not spread diseases.

Gretchen did not feel comforted by that information, as she tried not to itch the long-lasting sores on her neck and arms. She had survived bad guys in Costa Rica, mysteries at the Grand Canyon, and becoming an art-cart teacher only to be tortured by quarter-inch pests. She wondered what the next year would bring. She hoped that there would be no other *little* surprises.

ABOUT THE AUTHOR

Kathy Carman Henderson considers her life an adventure of its own. She was born in the Philippines, raised in Central Kansas, and spent much of her adult life following her husband's pastoral career through Iowa and Illinois. She herself was an art teacher and a Future Problem Solving coach for many years. Though this book is fiction, she used the journey she had with her own parents for inspiration.

Other titles from her include:

Fiction:
Costa Rican Adventure with Ben and Gretchen
Grand Canyon Adventure with Ben and Gretchen
Buck

Inspirational:
Party of the Ages

Stories to Learn and Draw by:
The Walking Vegetables
The One You Don't See Coming
The Tiger's Whisker
A Mouse's Wedding
The Ant and the Grasshopper

For Future Problem Solving International:
Treffinger, Don. **Tools for Problem Solvers,** (Kathy was a
contributing author)

Books illustrated for author Edna Creekmore Carman:
A Day of Rest
Tender Twig

And several coloring books.

Isaiah 58:11
" And the LORD shall guide thee continually, and satisfy thy
soul in drought, and make fat thy bones: and thou shalt be like
a watered garden, and like a spring of water, whose waters fail
not."
KJV

Made in the USA
Columbia, SC
01 May 2020